The Oracle

of Orvieto

By Russ Breault

Russ Breault

Acknowledgements

I would like to thank the following for their help and support in creating this work: To my long-time friend and mentor, Jim Pace; thanks for being my cheerleader and believer in this project from the very first draft. To Leah Shaver who helped edit the final draft and assisted in publication. To Reverend Jim Weathers for your helpful theological input. To my Delta friends who helped make the characters look and sound like real pilots: Jamie Bosworth, Bill Wiley, and Bob Carson. Thanks to Moe and Susan of Tea Fusions who provided the catalyst for the book by opening their humble tea shop to Sunday night Bible studies. Thanks also to Terry and Wanda Jennings, Brian Kaiser, Eric Stogner, Janeen Jamison, Jacqueline Wilk, Shirley Hill, and Mick Wilson who all read early drafts of this work and offered helpful advice. Thanks to Peachtree City for creating a wonderful place to live and work. Thanks to the Log House Men's group for your prayerful support. Lastly but most importantly, thanks to my wife Donna for putting up with the long and tedious process of sleepless nights and what probably seemed like incoherent babbling as the story and characters came to life in my mind. And of course, thanks and praise be to God, the true author of this work.

Dedication

This book is dedicated to all who seek truth and a good story.

This book is also dedicated to all my Delta friends who fly the jets that have taken me around the world.

And lastly, I dedicate this book to my six grandkids who one day might read this book: Leah, Abigail, Peyton, Isaac, Finley and Josephine.

Definition of "Oracle"

As a Message: (*n.*) The communications, revelations, or messages delivered by God to the prophets; also, the entire sacred Scriptures—usually in the plural.

As a Place: (*n.*) The sanctuary, or Most Holy place in the temple; also, the temple itself.

As a Person: (*n.*) One who communicates a divine command; an angel; a prophet.

"oracle." *Webster's Revised Unabridged Dictionary*. MICRA, Inc. 31 May. 2009.
Dictionary.com http://dictionary.classic.reference.com/browse/oracle

An Oracle can be a message, a person, and a place.
The Oracle of Orvieto is all three.

Chapter 1:

Darkness over the Deep

First Officer Brian Michaels sat deep in thought as they neared cruising altitude. The cockpit was well lit and enhanced by a myriad of control lights and display panels. The captain, Tom Jennings, was scanning the horizon. The relief first officer, Mitch Carson rounded out the three-man crew and was sitting in the jump seat. Brian looked out the right-side window of the Boeing 767 trying to see the Atlantic Ocean swirling six miles below. A layer of clouds shrouded his view. An occasional tanker or cargo ship might be chugging below, but he wouldn't have seen it. Despite freezing air shooting by at 600 mph and two huge Pratt and Whitney turbines pushing up to 62,000 pounds of thrust, it was amazingly quiet in the cockpit. Only the sound of the jet's ventilation system could be heard.

A slight smile came to Brian's face as he reminisced. He had been a Domestic First Officer flying the 757 and finally achieved the seniority to fly international on the 767. After a few weeks of simulators and flight training, it was now a reality. This was his first official Atlantic crossing in the cockpit (technically the "flight deck," but Brian was holding on to the old vernacular).

As they pierced the sky heading towards Rome, his thoughts wandered back to Atlanta. His wife Maryanne would be sleeping that night with the TV on low. Any time Brian was gone on a trip, she would leave it on for comfort. She missed his presence, his breathing, his warmth, his arms—everything. But over the years she learned to adjust to the frequent absences.

Hyler, their eight-year-old daughter, would always write a note to her dad before a trip and hide it in his flight case where he would find it later. It always said the same thing: "I love you sooooooo much!" Brian felt for the note in his left shirt pocket. It was a point of contact with the ones he loved as he raced towards another continent. He had a stack of Hyler's notes at home and it always reminded him of how often he was gone. Now he was gone again–this time halfway around the world.

Being a pilot was a good job. That's about all he could say about it. The perks were nice. Advancing to international gave him an opportunity to see more than just Memphis or Miami. Brian was in his mid-forties and had already been flying for twenty years. The first ten were in the Air Force. Flying a commercial jet is interesting but it doesn't compare with flying an F-16 rocket pulling up to 9Gs, reaching thirty thousand feet in minutes. Now that's flying! Nothing compares with the adrenaline rush. No passengers to worry about. Just you and whatever the machine could handle and boy, could it handle. He missed the high-flying days in the Air Force. At one point he was stationed in Afghanistan and flew out of Bagram Air Base. There were Taliban hostiles on the ground, but anti-aircraft fire was of little concern; it was impossible to reach the high altitudes where the "vipers" roam. The real threat was the mountainous terrain, and a shoulder fired SAM (Surface-to-Air Missile). The irony is that it was probably made in the USA and stolen from an American base or smuggled in from somewhere else.

Along with the adrenaline, he missed the camaraderie of his unit. Now, every time he flies, it's with a different pilot, most likely one he has never met. Conversations are cordial, but there is rarely any real bonding. Since Atlanta is such an enormous hub, there are hundreds of pilots in the international pool. They know when the trip is over it may be months or years before they fly together again. It was the luck of the draw. It's not like being with his squadron at Bagram. Those pilots would be friends for life.

The Air Force was a season full of expectation and excitement. He was much younger then, with no wife or children to distract. Bruce Springsteen called them the "Glory Days" and that is what they were. The only adrenaline rush now is when something goes wrong. A pilot friend once described the life of a commercial pilot as "endless days of boredom punctuated by a few brief moments of sheer terror." Brian remembered the time when his 737, in the middle of a torrential downpour, landed in Baton Rouge. Half-way down the runway it spun completely around as the jet hydroplaned off into the field. No injuries, just a whole lot of jitters. It was not the kind of adrenaline he was longing for! No disciplinary action was taken; his punishment was to be remanded back to the simulators for three days.

All the pilots were required to be in the flight deck until they achieved top-of-climb from take-off and just prior to descent for landing. It usually works out to be the first and last thirty minutes of an international flight. The trip from Atlanta to Rome is a little over ten hours. Not counting the half-hour for take-off and landing, the rest of the trip is divided into three-hour segments. The "pilot flying" would generally take two of the three segments but another pilot would take control on the way back. They achieved a cruising altitude of 37,000 feet. Tom was starting to move around and would take the first break. Brian would be the "pilot flying" and was happy for the opportunity since it was his first international flight. Mitch would be the "pilot monitoring."

"Brian, you've got the helm. I'm going to get some shut eye. Wake me in three hours and we'll trade places. Good night."

"I got her, captain."

"Get some rest, Tom. Maybe tomorrow if either of you are up to it, we can check out a few places in Rome." Brian said as Tom was moving toward the cockpit door.

"Maybe. I'll let you know how I feel." Tom yawned as he crawled off to the first-class cabin where a seat was waiting for him just in front of the curtain leading to coach. Tom was in his fifties and pretty burned out on international runs. *He may just want to stay in his hotel room and sleep*, Brian thought.

Mitch chimed in, "Count me out, Brian, I've arranged to spend the day with an Army friend of mine stationed here in Italy, maybe next time." Brian knew there probably wouldn't be a next time.

He went back to his thoughts. He had only known Tom and Mitch for a few hours. It was Brian's first time to Rome and he wasn't about to waste it. He had a 24-hour layover and planned to use it with or without a companion. Asking one of the flight attendants was out of the question. Maryanne would be miffed if she ever found out. She was a firm believer in the Reagan doctrine: "Trust but verify."

Brian met Maryanne right after leaving the Air Force. He had been living in Macon, Georgia where the rent was cheap and not too far from Warner Robbins AFB, where he had to report as part of the Air National Guard. Plus, it was

10

close enough to Atlanta, where he was waiting to see if Delta would hire him on as a commercial pilot. In the meantime, he was taking classes at Mercer University–no sense in wasting the GI bill. Everything was in transition and wasn't sure what he wanted to do. A course on European history through the Renaissance sounded interesting. He would go to the cafeteria to study. Not living on campus—it was the easiest thing to do. It was only a few weeks into the Fall semester when his life began to change.

He spotted Maryanne in the food line. She was older than most other students and that was good. Dating a girl fresh out of high school was out of the question. He watched her from the table. She was a stunner, about 5'7" in height, slender with an athletic build, light brown hair that settled on her shoulders but with eyes so blue you could see them across the room. As she slid her tray near the cashier, Maryanne turned her head and saw Brian gazing at her. She smiled. Brian knew he was caught but acted nonchalant and just turned his eyes back into the book. Maryanne was intrigued with Brian too for all the same reasons. Brian could also turn a head or two at 6 feet tall, muscular with short cropped brown hair and his own set of steely blue eyes. She sat down at a table not too far away, but close enough to be approachable if the guy had any nerve. Brian didn't miss the cue.

Getting up from his seat and quietly walking up to the table where her back was turned to him, he came alongside of where she was sitting and said, "Hi, my name is Brian and I'll be your server today. May I get you a cup of coffee to go with that lovely meal?"

She laughed. "No but you can sit down and talk to me. There aren't many students my age in here." They were both in their early thirties.

Brian sat down across from her. Maryanne was talkative and took the lead. "So, what are you studying? I saw you here the other day too."

Wow! She had her eyes on me before I ever laid eyes on her, Brian thought. "I'm just taking a course on European history. Actually... I'm really waiting to see if Delta is going to open up for me, I just got out of the Air Force."

Maryanne's mind was turning. *Here is a good-looking guy, my age, who is hoping to be a commercial pilot. Finally, someone with a real prospect for success...* she thought.

"That sounds like a pretty good plan," she said. "Actually, this is my second stab at school. The first time, I couldn't figure out what to do. After a few dead-end office jobs, I decided teaching would be more interesting and a lot more stable. So here I am... again." She cocked her head to the side and smiled. It was a smile that could melt ice. There

12

was something different about this girl… and it wouldn't take long for his head to catch up with his heart.

Brian and Maryanne started dating and love wasted no time to reach full bloom—a spring wedding and by July, Delta called with the good news. Maryanne would eventually finish her degree at the Mercer campus in Atlanta while Brian trained and trained and trained. After three months, he was co-pilot on a 737 flying short domestic hops. Two years later, Hyler would arrive and change their lives again.

Brian's mind focused back on the cockpit. No warning lights—a quick check for their altitude, direction and air speed—all systems normal. Tom had another hour to sleep; Mitch was cross checking the flight plan on the company iPad.

Everything was good. They were approaching the first waypoint. At every ten degrees of longitude, they were required to submit a *position report* to air traffic control in either Gander (Canada) or Shanwick (UK). They would be reporting to Gander until they got halfway across at 30 degrees west longitude. The position report is automatically submitted by way of a digital data link. The high frequency radio is now only used as a backup.

The data link would provide POSITION—TIME—ALTITUDE and then POSITION—TIME—POSITION. The first set of numbers gave their current location; the second set indicated when they were expected to be at the next waypoint and the coordinates of the waypoint after that—current-next-next. Delta Flight Control in Atlanta would then know where they were and where they expected to be. In the event something happened, God forbid, they would know where to look.

Precise rules and procedures make air travel safe. Standardized communication eliminates confusion.

The details of the flight plan were worked out earlier. Not much else to do until the next position report. Brian looked up into the night sky. The Milky Way Galaxy was putting on a spectacular display of stars rarely seen from the ground. In most parts of the world, light pollution has eliminated one of life's simplest pleasures—beholding the universe in all its grandeur. *How can there not be a God?* Brian thought. He imagined what it would look like from the International Space Station. Magnificent would be an understatement.

"Mitch, have you ever seen anything so beautiful?" Brian asked.

"Yeah, I agree, it never gets old. I've seen pictures from Hubble that just blow my mind. The pics coming from the James Webb telescope are even more incredible." Mitch concurred.

14

Mitch was a quiet type, so conversation was limited. That was okay, Brian didn't mind being alone in his thoughts. There was plenty to think about.

His mind returned to Maryanne. She was the best thing that ever happened to him and with perfect timing too. As a pilot in the Air Force, he never really wanted to settle down and was happy with short flings. Most women were looking for commitment, but Brian was only looking for some fun and a little companionship. But something changed upon leaving the military. It was as if a switch flipped on in his head and was ready for the real thing. Maryanne was it.

Brian thought about all the changes in his life. Sometimes life progresses gradually and then other times it happens quickly. Transitional events seem to happen suddenly, like meeting Maryanne or getting out of the Air Force. Today it's one thing and tomorrow everything is different. One day an officer and the next day a civilian, one day lonely and the next day in love. One day a student and the next day a pilot for Delta, one day a husband and the next day a father.

What Brian didn't know were the changes that were yet to come, changes that would begin in just a few hours, changes that would start him on a quest that men and women over the centuries had died for: the quest of every seeking soul. It would begin in Rome, the cradle of Western Civilization.

Chapter 2:

And Then There Was Light

Light was dawning over Europe as the jet drew closer to land. Brian had just come back on the flight deck from a three-hour nap. Tom was the "pilot flying" for the last leg as they prepared for descent. The flight attendants were finishing up their breakfast service as the passengers roused from fitful sleep.

"Hey Brian, get any sleep?" Tom asked.

"Not really, someone was snoring so loud, it kept the whole cabin awake." Brian said with obvious irritation. "I wanted to dump a glass of water on him... I tried to bribe one of the flight attendants, but she wouldn't do it. It's hard to find good help." Brian said now laughing.

"Brian, I know you want to go off somewhere today, but the mattress is calling me, and I feel compelled to obey. Sorry..."

"That's fine Tom, no problem. I'll figure something out."

The sight of the sun shining horizontally through the clouds was spectacular. The huge orange orb lit up the horizon with an array of brilliant colors. The atmosphere diffused the light enough to look straight at it. Now over land, Brian could see the lights of cities and towns where it was still night, but up here, six miles high, it was morning, and it was beautiful. The earth below would remain dark for another hour. *This is going to be a great day!* Brian told himself... even if he did go solo.

The landing was uneventful. Walking down the concourse, Brian saw an old friend from the Air Force now flying for United Airlines and based in Chicago. He hadn't seen Jim Covino in years.

"Tom, I'll see you at the hotel, I need to catch up with someone."

"Suit yourself, it will cost you—the shuttle is free."

"It's worth it... nothing like the glory days!"

Brian walked over to where Jim was standing. "Hey, don't I know you?" Brian asked with a smile.

"Hey Brian... it's good to see you." Jim said with a voice that seemed flat.

Brian shrugged it off. "Got a few minutes? The Pilot lounge is right there." He pointed across the concourse.

They dodged a stream of travelers and walked across to the pilot's lounge. "Jim, it's so good to see you." Brian said as they sat down at a small table. "I haven't talked to you since Afghanistan."

"Yeah" he said slowly. "I got on with United about the same time you did with Delta. The past few years have been pretty rough. Courtney and I didn't make it. I don't know what happened, things just fell apart. I guess it was the constant travel. Adjusting to all the absences was too stressful. I have two boys; Adam is twelve now and Jake is ten. I hardly ever see them." He swallowed and looked down at his feet. He looked back at Brian after a few seconds. "Courtney has custody, but I get 'em every other weekend. Thankfully she still lives in the Chicago area. How about you? Is your life any better?"

Brian was almost regretting he ever started the conversation. He just wanted to reminisce about the old days with his unit—maybe catch up on some other friends he hadn't seen in a while. He wasn't expecting all this.

"Maryanne and I are doing fine. We have an eight-year-old daughter named Hyler. It's an old family name, it's my mother-in-law's maiden name, but we liked it as a first name. Maryanne miscarried our second and then it just didn't happen again. It was not for lack of trying!" He said trying to lighten the conversation. "We decided not to go with fertility

19

drugs. The thought of triplets or more was just too scary. But we have a good life. I'm sorry things didn't work out with you and Courtney."

"Yeah, I'll just be glad when all this crap is over." The bitterness in Jim's voice was palpable. He didn't acknowledge anything Brian said about his family, it was like he didn't hear him and was consumed with his own misery. Life had beaten him down and Brian could offer nothing to help.

It was time to go. "Jim, it was good catching up with you." Brian lied. "I hope things look up for you soon."

"Yeah, me too. Thanks for taking the time to chat. See ya somewhere…"

They left the pilot lounge and went in opposite directions, Jim towards the gate and Brian towards customs. Walking slowly down the concourse feeling depressed, he hated to see Jim in such a dismal state. They had such great times in the Air Force together, but Jim was a completely different person now, and it wasn't for the better.

Brian shook it off and focused back on the day ahead with a plan to experience the joys of Italy. His spirits gradually rose again and thought about being a tourist in a city jam packed with more history and culture than could be imagined. Brian was in a foreign country—and like everyone else—was required to show a valid passport and present his bags for inspection.

Customs was a breeze, but the taxi ride to the hotel where the crew would be spending the night was different... in fact, it was crazy. It was the morning rush hour—all the traffic and noise of a huge city with no lines on the road to tell what lane you were in. Cars, trucks, and scooters seemed to dart in and out and merge together at intersections like some kind of organized anarchy. *I can fly a jet, but this traffic is scary!* Brian thought.

It was still early in the morning. Checking in at the hotel was easier than what he had braced for. The woman at check-in spoke English well; it was the thick Italian accent that slowed down Brian's comprehension. She had a smooth dark complexion with long wavy brown hair and a nametag that said "Emanuella." She laughed as Brian struggled to understand, not knowing any Italian except for "ciao."

Brian had the rest of the day to explore Rome. Locating the room, he threw the roller bag on the bed. *Walk-in closets are bigger than this room!* Brian thought. It was time to consult the tour book. Where to start? The Vatican and Saint Peter's? The Sistine Chapel is there too. What about the Catacombs? Or maybe the ruins of the Colosseum or some ancient pagan temples? It's not every city that has two thousand years of history. Not far from where Julius Caesar would have stood in the Forum to address the crowds was a medieval fortress built fourteen hundred years later. This place was a timeline of civilization. Brian started to remember bits and pieces from his course on European history.

Flying international would make Rome a frequent stop and so he did not have to rush out and see all the typical tourist sites today. A different approach was called for—start with the obscure and work his way up the tourist top ten list. Trading the uniform for blue jeans, sneakers and a golf shirt, Brian had "American tourist" written all over him.

How do you begin with something less prominent, perhaps something not even in the tour book? *Emanuella, she might have some ideas*, he thought. Brian came out of the elevator and scanned the front desk to locate her but she was nowhere to be seen. Standing in the back of the check-in area, he finally noticed her coming out from behind the partition wall that separates the front desk from the business office in the back. Brian caught her attention.

"Emanuella, can I bother you for minute?" She smiled politely. She didn't know what "bother" meant in that context and wasn't sure what to expect. "I will have many opportunities to come to Rome over the next year" he said quickly. "And I want to see everything, but I don't want to start with all the typical tourist sites. Is there something really unique you could point me to for today?"

Emanuella smiled. She was relieved he wasn't asking her out on a date or something. "I have just the place if you can give it a full day." Brian nodded that he could. "Orvieto. It is only about an hour by train toward Florence. It is a medieval town that sits high on a mountain bluff. It is like dropping into a time capsule right out of the Middle Ages. Apart from electricity and a few cars, it is the same as it was five hundred years ago. You will love it. By the way, if you go, be sure to check out Saint Patrick's Well."

"That's perfect!" Brian shouted and then caught himself. She laughed. "What is so special about a well?" he asked.

"You will find it, and you will know why when you get there." Brian was curious now. Nothing like a little mystery to spice up the day.

Walking outside the hotel, he hailed a cab to the train station, navigated the language barrier, and bought a ticket for Orvieto. He picked up his cell phone and left a voice mail with Tom Jennings.

"Tom, this is Brian… just wanted to let you know I'm taking a train to Orvieto and will be back tonight around 6:00. Have a good day." Click.

It was something pilots and crew would always do as a precaution when someone goes off alone. The train was departing in 20 minutes. He was jazzed about seeing the Italian countryside from the ground. This layover was going to be one to remember.

Brian sat down in a window seat and waited for the train to move. It was time to read about his destination.

Chapter 3:

Orvieto

According to historians, Orvieto's history predates even that of Rome and was first settled by the Etruscans around 900 BC. This early pagan culture was later assimilated into ancient Rome in 280 BC. For almost thirty centuries, Orvieto has been desirable as a defensible stronghold with a fortified wall surrounding the entire city. A long winding road ascends nearly a thousand feet to the top with nothing outside the wall except a steep drop sure to kill any invader who lost his grip. The rocky bluff forms a vertical cascade to the valley below featuring some of the most beautiful farmland in all of Italy—lush with vineyards and orchards watered by the Paglia River.

Fascination had set in. Other than his travels in the Airforce, Brian hadn't really ventured abroad. The rich history and culture of Old Europe was casting its spell as it has for so many that come from the New World for the first time.

They were well outside of Rome. Brian looked up from his book and began to take in the view. Wildflowers had transformed the rolling countryside into a palette of color. Brian's eyes were drawn upward to the tops of the surrounding hills. He could see ancient walled towns perched high above the valley where the train was speeding to the next stop. A silver blue haze settled like a blanket and created a soft, peaceful and almost mystical quality. Occasionally he would spot an old monastery or convent. Mountains and hills, streams and valleys, with terraced vineyards, orchards and miles of olive groves, it was more beautiful than he had imagined.

The train pulled into the Orvieto station right on schedule. No worry about getting back; 16 trains pass through to Rome every day. He had the rest of the day and wasn't going to be rushed. It was a small station. Only one other passenger stepped off. She walked over to where the public shuttle would stop and then trek back up the mountain. Brian followed her to the covered bench where two others were waiting. He couldn't read the signs–there was no English anywhere. Hating to ask, "Excuse me, do you speak English?"

"You are in luck. How can I help you?" She said in near perfect English. Brian was elated. The language barrier can be daunting and an hour outside of Rome, hearing anything other than Italian becomes a rare commodity. She looked to be in her mid thirties, petite, with short dark hair.

"Can you tell me how often the shuttle bus runs?"

"Every half-hour, so we still have about fifteen minutes to wait."

26

That was too long. He had to make the most of this day. "Would you like to share a cab with me?" he asked. There were two cabs parked by the train station. Both drivers were leaning on the side of the first cab smoking cigarettes.

"Sure" she said with a smile. "You seem like a nice enough guy; besides, I don't meet many Americans."

They walked toward the first cab and motioned they were together. The station was several miles from town and took about twenty minutes. When they reached the base of the mountain the way became steep. Five minutes later, the road flattened out. They passed through a massive gate. The car rumbled and vibrated on ancient cobblestone as it came to a stop not far from the city entrance.

The woman's name was Maria Marinelli. *I bet half the women in Italy are named Maria.* Brian thought. She was a professional woman, owned a local travel agency and was also on a municipal committee to promote tourism. That explained why she spoke English so well. It was a stroke of luck to meet her, or so he thought.

"Would you be up for a cup of coffee while I ask you a few more questions?" he asked with a hopeful smile.

She was hesitant, not because of him but because of work that was piling up at the office. "I can spare a few minutes, but I really need to get back to the office soon. I

27

hadn't planned on going to Rome yesterday and now I'm behind."

It was mid-May. The temperature was perfect; the clouds he saw flying into Rome had disappeared. A gentle breeze blew through his clothes and seemed to flap with excitement for what this day might bring.

He paused to take in his surroundings and was awestruck by the medieval time capsule that surrounded him. Not far from the taxi stand was an outdoor café. It wasn't too crowded. Brian and Maria quickly found a seat.

Orvieto has a population of about ten thousand. The main industry in town is tourism. In the valley, it's agriculture and wine making. Most of the tourists are from Europe. For some reason, Orvieto is largely undiscovered by Americans. Maria was hoping to change that.

"Maria, I have to tell you how enchanted I am with Italy. Orvieto is wonderfully quaint, and I have only been here for two minutes! I can't wait to explore the town." he exclaimed.

Maria was pleased. After all, he was the kind of tourist she was hoping to attract. *Nothing beats word of mouth!* she thought.

The waiter came over and took their order, two coffees… Brian ordered a cappuccino and Maria asked for her usual, espresso with a little sugar.

"Where should I start my tour? I have about six hours before I need to head back."

Towering above the roofs of shops and restaurants, he could see the top of a large structure. "Well, you can't miss the cathedral." she pointed. "It's the center of everything, and is one of the most beautiful gothic cathedrals in Europe. It features mosaics on both outside and inside of the church, which you don't often see. Construction began in 1290. You should also see the Papal Palace. After that, just enjoy the town itself with all the unique shops and narrow streets." she offered.

"Oh, and another idea, if you can find someone to take you down, there are miles of tunnels underground that were built during Roman times. They were designed to be a means of escape in case of attack. There are scheduled tours, check at the Palace for when the next one leaves." she said while standing up from the table. "I really must get going, it was good to meet you, if you come back, please look me up." She handed him her card; *Umbria Travel* was her company. Umbria was the name of the province, one of twenty in Italy. As she turned to leave, she said, "Something else you might find interesting is Saint Patrick's Well. Some people have unique experiences there. It appears Pope Clement pronounced a special blessing on it when they began construction. I guess you must be open to it."

"I'm open for anything today! Thanks again for all your help." Brian put ten Euros on the table and ventured off toward the Duomo (from the Latin meaning "House of God").

Chapter 4:

Enchantment

There was still plenty of time; it was only mid-morning. Brian strolled slowly toward the narrow street that led to the cathedral with shops lining both sides. Unable to resist, he went into the first store. It had just opened and was filled with colorful pottery, cooking implements, wine, aprons, t-shirts and more filling the shelves and, of course, the obligatory rack of postcards. There was time to buy all that later—what he needed was a map. A pilot always likes to know where he is going. Navigation is part of the training! A detailed street map was waiting for him in a small display rack near the window. The purchase was completed with gestures and a smile. Stepping back into the street, he mixed with a small stream of tourists flowing in the same direction.

A wide courtyard area soon emerged anchored by an enormous Duomo. Having seen St. Patrick's in New York, Brian found this entirely different. Graced with encrusted marble on the outside with gothic style mosaics covering the entire front face of the structure, it was amazingly colorful. Brian was mesmerized knowing it was over 600 years old. Three massive bronze doors covered with bas relief sculptures surrounded by concentric arches led the way inside. He entered through the center door and was struck with the height of the ceiling and all the wonderfully intricate frescoes featuring one biblical scene after another across the entire top of the structure. Like seeing the Rocky Mountains or the Grand Canyon for the first time, he was in awe. Slowly moving toward the left wall, he could hear the sound of shoes and muted whispers echoing throughout the cavernous space. Against the wall were more intricate bas-relief scenes sculpted out of wood representing the Acts of the Apostles. As his eyes moved up the towering facade, it transitioned to colorful mosaics then merged near the top with brilliant stained-glass windows roughly a hundred feet above the floor—all telling the story in hand-crafted pictures by the greatest artisans of the medieval era.

Lessons from Sunday school came to life through the deep mist of dormant memories. Pivotal scenes were painted, carved, etched in stained glass or painstakingly put together in a mosaic made from thousands of pieces of melted Venetian glass. There was Mary and Joseph with the holy infant, Jesus teaching in the synagogue at age twelve, John baptizing him in the Jordan, Jesus calling his disciples, teaching the parable of the lost sheep, calming the storm, raising Lazarus from the dead, travailing in the Garden of Gethsemane, crucified, risen from the dead, and declared the King of Kings. Each scene seemed to rekindle a story remembered from youth group.

Feeling overwhelmed, it was too much to take in at one time. After twenty minutes he returned to the courtyard. Outside was what might be described as an enormous patio that went from the steps of the cathedral to the street. It was at least 150 feet long and 200 feet wide across the entire front of the cathedral. Where the street met the courtyard, many of the locals brought their own chairs and lined up along the sidewalk or in groups on the patio. People were just setting up as they congregated in the shade of the great structure, playing games, drinking wine and enjoying life. It was a central gathering place, especially during *siesta*.

That's another thing Brian had to learn about Europe; in most small towns, people took siesta seriously! From 2:00 to 5:00 in the afternoon, many shops and restaurants would close but reopen again for the evening. He hadn't figured on that and was hoping it wouldn't interfere with his plans.

Brian fumbled for the map–it was time to start being more strategic. What did Maria say... something about tunnels? He located the Papal Palace; it was right next to the cathedral and didn't realize it.

The Palace was a beauty of Gothic design but small and simple compared to the Duomo. It was now a municipal museum. Several Popes in the past either stayed at the Palace on occasion or lived here as the need arose, taking refuge during times of contention with the emperor or some other political adversary. He took a few minutes to read the descriptive panels along the wall offered in multiple languages. Apparently, the construction of the Papal Palace was begun by Pope Urban IV in 1261 and completed in 1297. It took 30 years, but the work was not continuous. It proceeded in spurts as money and manpower was available. New design ideas and subsequent costly modifications slowed the process as well. In fact, most ancient structures throughout Europe were modified, extended, and reshaped over the centuries as different architects sold their ideas to the reigning bishop. Sweeping changes also occurred as architecture transitioned from Romanesque to Gothic during the thirteenth and fourteenth centuries.

Brian was fascinated. There was nothing this old in Atlanta or in Nashville where he grew up. Reading on, the Romanesque style was common to southern Europe and dominated from the ninth through twelfth centuries. It was heavy construction, using brick and masonry with rounded domes and arches with only a few small windows for light. Gothic style had come in from France in the twelfth century and dominated through the sixteenth century. The new French style had a much brighter interior with higher ceilings, large stained-glass windows and angular arches. Flying buttresses were introduced to counter the weight of the towering structure so the walls wouldn't collapse. The Duomo began as a Romanesque design in 1290 and ended up Gothic by the time it was completed in 1330.

Brian approached the salesclerk at the museum store.

"Do you speak English?"

"Yes, a little." she replied.

"What can you tell me about the tunnels under the city? Can they be seen?"

Looking at a paper kept under the counter, "I'm sorry; they are not doing tours today. They are temporarily closed for repairs."

Brian was disappointed. The tunnels sounded interesting. "What can you tell me about St. Patrick's Well?"

Her eyes brightened. "I think you will like that; it is very popular, and it is open today. You should go."

Brian contemplated her response. Her eyes went wide. In fact, her entire expression changed when he mentioned the well. *What is so special about this thing and why was it named after Saint Patrick?* Brian thought. He picked up a brochure in English and started reading.

Saint Patrick lived in Ireland during the fifth century and never visited Orvieto. Why this well was named after him a thousand years later is curious. Apparently, Patrick periodically escaped to Station Island in the middle of Lough Derg, a lake in Northern Ireland fed by the River Shannon. On this island was a cave in the ground so deep that he called it Purgatory. Patrick had prayed for a way to bring the Word of God to Ireland and convert the Irish people. Drawn to Station Island by the need for prayer and solitude, Patrick wrote about having extraordinary experiences. Legend has it that Jesus appeared to him there. Descending into the cave, Patrick described having dramatic encounters with both angels and demons. Were they visions, apparitions or real manifestations? No one knows for sure. It was said that anyone who could hold out in the cave for a day and a night would be purged of sins and be allowed to "see the torment of the damned and the joys of the blessed." Early Christianity had adopted a strong view of penance as a way of paying for sins. *Guilt must be a powerful motivator*, Brian thought. Patrick succeeded in evangelizing all of Ireland! People would make pilgrimages to the island and would fast for days before going. If they could endure a night in the cave they would emerge spiritually renewed. A twelfth century English monk supposedly found the cave and had a similar experience. The legend of the cave spread throughout Europe and even inspired Dante's Inferno in the early 1300s. Curiously, Pope Alexander VI had the cave closed in 1497 due to complaints that it was no longer producing spiritual visions. Brian laughed when he read that. *No more visions? Ha! I'll show you,* he thought.

Brian was trying to piece it together. In 1527, Pope Clement VII commissioned the well to be built in Orvieto 30 years after Saint Patrick's cave was closed. He wondered if the well was named after Saint Patrick because it resembled a deep hole in the ground. *Or did people have unique spiritual encounters there?* No one really seemed to understand why it was named after Saint Patrick. Growing up Baptist, he didn't know anything about Purgatory, but he believed in God. Three people had mentioned the well today, and Maria even referred to people having strange experiences. Brian's curiosity was piqued and was eager to continue reading.

At this time in Europe, there was a power balance between the Pope, the Emperor and various kings. The Emperor, Charles the Fifth, was not Italian and therefore established his seat of power in Spain, rather than Rome. Other national and religious stakeholders were concerned he was getting too powerful. Many felt the Papacy was coming under "imperial domination" and feared the Pope would lose his ability to act and rule the Church independent of imperial manipulation. In 1526, the League of Cognac was formed, which included France, Milan, Venice, Florence and the Vatican (Italy as it exists today was not a united country until 1861). The Pope threw his support to France. This meant war. Charles defeated the French armies stationed in Italy but ran out of money to pay the troops. Some thirty-four thousand German mercenary soldiers hired by the emperor formed a mutiny against Charles and decided to march on Rome. They were determined to get paid one way or another and there was plenty to plunder in Rome. With merely five thousand Papal troops protecting the city, it only took a day for the mercenaries to breach the walls and begin their rampage of theft and destruction. Thanks to the Swiss guards protecting Saint Peter's, Pope Clement was spared and later escaped to safety by disguising himself as a fruit vendor. He ended up in Orvieto and commissioned the building of the well in 1527.

Charles was fiercely opposed to the Reformation and the influence of Martin Luther that began ten years earlier in 1517. As a devout Catholic, he feared the spread of Protestantism would be divisive and make it more difficult to rule effectively. With the nailing of Luther's 95 Theses of Contention on the door of the castle church in Wittenberg, Germany, Luther began a revolution of religious thought based on the Bible instead of tradition and Church mandate. Ironically, many of the pillaging troops were sympathetic to Luther's complaints against the Catholic Church including the pressure selling of indulgences to commoners who could ill afford it. Indulgences allegedly offered forgiveness of personal sins and even secured a loved one's release from Purgatory. They were conned into believing that every dollar given to the Church knocked a year off their stay in Purgatory. They could also do the same for relatives. *Such a deal! It sounded like a spiritual debt relief program.* Brian thought.

The Church also imposed harsh tax policies to support the ecclesiastical bureaucracy in their own country as well as the Vatican. Pressure tactics intensified in the early 1500s to fund the building of Saint Peter's, which began in 1506. By 1526, the soldiers, mostly German commoners, were tired and angry over the abuse. Luther had struck a nerve. The troops were more than happy to loot Rome; the city they felt had been looting them for years.

Brian looked up from the literature found at the Palace and was drawn back to the present. It was all so fascinating. Scanning the map to locate the well, it was not too far and would only take ten minutes on foot. He plotted his route through the narrow side streets that were barely wide enough for one of the Fiats that dominated Italian roads.

Up ahead was a small microvan making a delivery. It was parked beside a bakery with just enough room for him to walk past. The deliveryman was singing a lovely Italian melody as he went in and out of the truck stocking the shelves with fresh pastries and bread. Brian stopped a few yards away just to watch, listen and smell the aroma. The man smiled, tipped his head and never missed a note. Brian felt stress leaving his body. If there were a chair, he would sit right there. *What was this feeling?* Brian wondered. It was peaceful and content. No striving. Life slowed to be enjoyed in the moment.

Enchanting is the only word that came close. It was like cognac, rich and wonderful. He sipped it slow to make it last.

After about ten minutes the truck left for the next delivery. Brian started moving again. Up a hill and down the next, Orvieto was quaint beyond compare. Time stood still as his feet danced along the cobblestone. He had fallen into a fairy tale and was captivated to the core.

Chapter 5:

The Woman at the Well

A small group of people were gathering for the next tour down into Saint Patrick's Well. It was covered by a large round brick building with an open roof for sunlight to illuminate the shaft. Brian had about ten minutes to wait. There were several kiosks of information that kindly offered a choice of languages—Italian, French, German, Spanish, and English—*thank goodness!* Brian loved learning how things came to be and how they worked. This incredible well took ten years to dig, is two hundred feet deep, and 42 feet wide. It was designed with two parallel stairways that wind all the way down to where the water can be accessed. Donkey carts with large barrels to carry water could descend on one stairway and ascend the other, yet never bump to each other. The kiosks described the stairs as a "double helix" design because it looks like a DNA molecule. Others have described it as a parallel corkscrew. As an artesian well, the water rises naturally from an underground aquifer. However, due to Orvieto's elevation, the well still needed to drop 200 feet, even from the city's lowest point. Orvieto's weakness as a defensible stronghold was not having a reliable source of water. When Pope Clement VII was here hiding out from Emperor Charles V after the

Sack of Rome, he commissioned the building of the well just in case.

This could be cool! Brian thought. As an engineering major in college, he was intrigued. People started lining up. There were only about ten waiting for the next tour and was standing behind a woman carrying a small briefcase. *She must be in town on business*, Brian thought, noticing a luggage tag dangling from the strap. *She's an American, maybe she knows some Italian too.* The kiosks may have been in several languages, but the tour guide was strictly local.

Brian leaned forward. "I see you're from the States. I saw your luggage tag. Do you know any Italian?" he ventured.

She turned and smiled. "Actually, I've been in Italy for over a year and have become pretty good with the language, but I'm not fluent yet. I'll be glad to translate if I can."

"That's great! By the way, my name is Brian Michaels."

"Nice to meet you, Brian, my name is Sarah... Sarah Foxworth. I'm from Dallas but I had a chance to transfer to Italy with my company. I work in international sales with Texas Instruments."

"It's fantastic that you can live here. I'm a pilot for Delta and fly back out tomorrow morning. This is my first time in Italy, and have been enthralled since I landed... can't get enough of this place!"

"I know just how you feel, I love it here."

The tour was beginning. They followed the guide through the door and Brian handed over the ticket he bought at the Palace. The guide offered a brief description in Italian of everything Brian already read. That was it; they were free to explore the well on their own. It was 248 steps to the bottom. With Brian's very first step down into the well, the prayers of Saint Patrick went to work. Maybe it was all the art and sculptures he saw at the Duomo. Maybe it was the sense of enchantment walking the narrow streets, but something spiritual was buzzing around in his soul. It was more than just random thoughts. It was deeper, much deeper, like the well he had just entered. Was this why it was named after Saint Patrick's Purgatory cave? The brochure mentioned that Jesus appeared to him there. Something was going on in this well.

Brian had grown up Baptist, as most everyone else in Nashville. He was involved with a youth group but drifted after high school and never really thought much about church from the moment he stepped foot onto the campus of UT in Knoxville. Wine, women and song was much more interesting. There were friends along the way in the Air Force and now in Atlanta who had invited him to church from time to time, but he just wasn't interested. He considered himself a

Christian, but Sundays were for sleep and golf. So why was he feeling this way? It was like a switch flipped on in his spirit that had never been turned on before.

With each step down into the well, the sensation became stronger. It wasn't scary or intimidating; it was just new and even intriguing yet also seemed like a longing or a kind of thirst. *What is this feeling?* Musings of God were just not normal for him... except when you behold the universe from over the Atlantic, how can you not think of God? He remembered what Maria told him. Is there something mystical about this well? Was he going to encounter angels and demons like Saint Patrick? Would there be a revelation of heaven and hell? Natural curiosity kept him going.

Sarah was a few feet in front. "Sarah, this may be a strange question, but I am getting some really weird spiritual vibes. I have never felt this way before. In fact, I don't consider myself a religious person. Do you feel anything or is it my imagination?"

"No, but maybe God is trying to get your attention. The well is a deeply spiritual metaphor. One of the most famous stories of Jesus is called The Woman at the Well. Wells are prominent in the Old Testament too; the most famous is Jacob's well, which is the same one where Jesus met the woman. The Bible also refers to our relationship with God as drawing from the wells of salvation for water that is clean and pure as compared to the polluted cisterns offered by worldliness and false religions. I guess my last thought would be Jesus saying that out of your innermost being would flow rivers of living water, flowing as it were from a well deep within us. He was referring to the Holy Spirit who comes to indwell the believer."

Brian didn't expect all that. "I thought you worked for Texas Instruments! How can you know so much? Are you a minister too?"

"No, but I've been in Bible studies for many years. Maybe it's my Texas roots, you know, the buckle of the Bible Belt." she laughed.

They continued their descent deeper into the well. It really was an amazing feat of engineering. Across the way and above them was the parallel stairway that led back up. There was no fear of falling into the well, as a thick wall separated the well shaft from the stairs. Despite it being a hole in the ground, there was plenty of light due to 72 windows that cut through to the inside shaft naturally lit from the sky above. Electric lights were added for more consistent illumination. Torches were used in centuries past. As they continued their descent, Brian's thoughts returned to the scenes in the Duomo and then back to the youth group and all the activities and retreats. He always believed in God but drifted away over time. Something was drawing him back.

"Sarah, this feeling keeps getting stronger the deeper we go. When you were talking, it was as if every word was oil being poured on a rusty hinge. Suddenly, I have a desire, no, not a desire, a need to reconnect with God. This is so weird. These thoughts are not normal for me."

"Brian, when was the last time you prayed?"

"I can't remember the last time. I'm sure a few prayers were said flying over Afghanistan, dodging bullets and mountains, but I don't remember."

"If God is trying to get your attention, why don't you take just a minute and ask him what he wants? Ask him to make himself known to you and see what happens."

Now Brian was starting to get nervous. "What if God has something bad to tell me? Maybe he is going to dump on me for all the lousy things I've done in my life or the way I have ignored him all these years."

"Brian that is not God's way. He may want you to be aware of your sins or your distance from him, so you will seek his forgiveness and change the direction of your life, but he does not condemn you. All of God's condemnation for sin was placed upon Jesus when he was nailed to the cross. That is what the crucifixion was all about. He took the entire penalty for our sins, a penalty that we deserved. It is because of the cross that we can be completely forgiven. All we must do is accept what he accomplished for us, ask for his forgiveness and ask to be filled with his Spirit. You can do it right now with a simple prayer."

Brian resisted. It sounded like a prepared speech. "What makes you think I'm not a Christian?" he said with obvious irritation.

Sarah knew the difference between a marginal and a committed believer. She had been a Christian in name—only for years. "Brian, it is not for me to judge your relationship with God. That is between you and Him. But I do know that the Bible says, *By their fruits you shall know them.* (Matt 7:20) Do you have peace? Do you have joy? Do you have confidence in your relationship with Christ? Do you pray? Do you ever read the Bible? Do you ever go to church? Paul says we are to examine ourselves. If you gave yourself a test of faith, would you pass? I am not trying to cast judgment on you but rather help you see that being a Christian affects every area of your life, not something you did 20 years ago and then forgotten again until Christmas or Easter."

Brian's mind was spinning. Is it just a coincidence that he encountered Sarah today? Over the past year, he and Maryanne have talked a few times about going back to church, mostly for Hyler. Sunday school would be good for her. They weren't very good at talking about God. *That was the job of the church*, Brian thought.

47

He reflected on Sarah's words but wasn't prepared to take that step. Maybe he wasn't a Christian after all. Why was he fighting this so much? If he was a believer, shouldn't he agree with her? Instead, he found himself resisting. It was like a tug of war going on in his mind or spirit or somewhere in between. There was a draw in the spirit, but something else within him was applying the brakes.

They continued deeper into the well. It was getting colder. The sound of footsteps and conversations echoed more the deeper they went. The stir in his spirit was getting deeper too and he thought about what Sarah said. The phrase "wells of salvation" kept coming back to mind.

There was a small landing a few steps down. "Sarah, wait a minute." She stopped at the landing. Brian was a few steps behind. "Okay, I think I need to pray. I can't shake this feeling. Why is it called *wells of salvation*? What does that mean?"

"Brian, many people in the secular world and those who subscribe to other religions may not agree with this, but salvation means you have been forgiven, your sins are no longer held against you because you have placed them on Christ by faith. It is what sets Christianity apart from every other belief system or philosophy. Nothing else offers a solution for sin. Sin is real. It is all around you and is responsible for all the ugliness and evil in the world. Some of that gunk resides in your soul. God hates sin but he loves people, including you. He demonstrated his love very clearly through the cross. Who else would willingly endure that kind of suffering? The cross means we never have to question whether God loves us."

Brian was caught up with what she was saying. Ordinarily he would have tuned it out, but for some reason he was ready to hear it. Sarah continued. "God wants to offer you two things. First, he wants to offer you a relationship with him right now by filling you with his Spirit. Second, he wants to offer you an eternity with him in heaven. But you can't receive either one until you ask Jesus into your life. He has already paid for everything through the cross. Then, and only then, can you stand before God totally clean and worthy of heaven. Then and only then can his Spirit dwell within your soul because your sins are no longer an obstacle. All it takes is a prayer." Sarah waited a minute for her words to sink in and then continued.

"The reason it is so hard for most people to get to this point is pride. We all want to do it our way, on our terms. Others might be afraid of changes that may occur in their lives. They have become comfortable in their lifestyles. Their sins have become like pets. They don't realize their pet sin is really like a rabid dog that will one day turn and maul them to death. We can't let the fear of change keep us from changing

49

for the good. We must believe anything God does for us is for our benefit and be willing to trust Him."

Brian was ready. The feeling inside his spirit was like a dam about to burst and didn't need any more convincing. "Sarah, you must lead those Bible studies because no one else has ever explained Christianity the way you just did. It sounds perfectly logical, and it never has before! What do I do now?"

Brian hit the mark. Not only did he ask the right question, but pegged Sarah for the expert she was. She had organized and led Bible studies for years before moving to Italy and had taken several postgraduate courses at Dallas Theological Seminary. But when she spoke to Brian, it wasn't with complicated theology, but as someone who had experienced the very thing Brian was going through. He was in good hands.

"Look, the other tourists have passed us by or gone back up. Stay right here and just ask Jesus into your life. Ask him to forgive you and ask him to fill you with his Holy Spirit. I will step down here while you have your time with God."

Brian looked through one of the 72 windows that brought light into the stairwell. Soon another light would be shining and this time it would be in his soul. He prayed exactly as Sarah described. As soon as he said, "Amen" a tremendous burden seemed to lift. The sense of urgency and longing that began earlier was gone and was suddenly replaced with peace. An unexplainable joy started to fill his soul and a smile that was ear to ear spread across his face. He felt lighter! It was like being in love, as if being embraced.

He hurried down to where Sarah was waiting for him. "Sarah! I can't believe it. I feel so different! I can't explain it, but I know Jesus came into my life. It feels like I'm floating in warm oil. Thank you so much for taking the time to help me."

"Brian, it was a blessing for me to help you, and I am glad you were receptive. Unfortunately, it is time for me to leave. I would love to spend more time with you, but I have an appointment in Rome this afternoon. Here is my card. Drop me an email if you have questions. Start praying, start reading the Bible, and when you get home, start going to church. Those three disciplines will keep you growing. God bless you, Brian." And with that she started back up the stairs and quickly disappeared at the first turn.

Brian felt alone, but not lonely. He stood motionless and didn't know whether to go up or down. He was whispering under his breath, "thank you Jesus" repeatedly. Catching himself, he realized that had never happened before, but it felt good saying it, as if it released something in his spirit. He started again whispering, "thank you Jesus, thank you for coming into my life." The sense of joy became euphoric.

Sarah Foxworth was climbing the stairs out of the well with a sense of elation at being able to help Brian into the kingdom. Suddenly she heard a voice say "stop!" She knew that voice; it was not an audible voice. It was a voice in her spirit. Sarah already knew what to do and had learned over the years to be obedient to that voice. Turning around, she went back down the stairs into the well. Brian hadn't moved from where she left him. It looked like he was talking to himself.

Brian turned to see who was coming and was excited to see who it was. "Sarah! I can't stop thanking Jesus for coming into my life. It seems the more I say it the more joy floods my soul. I feel like I'm going to explode!"

She was excited for him. She too had been born again many years ago and remembered how wonderful and life changing it was. Some people may call it a conversion experience. "Brian, I am so happy for you. What you are experiencing is the presence and fullness of the Holy Spirit. Bask in it. This sense of exhilaration may wane as you re-encounter the world, but your faith will never be the same. You have become a new creation in Christ. God's Spirit will never leave you and you can have these moments again if you seek it."

"Sarah, I believe you. When I fell in love with my wife, Maryanne, it was wonderful. My love for her was real and consuming. She was all I could think about. That's how I feel right now! It's like my soul has been infused with an overwhelming sense of joy and peace. It feels like being in love… except deeper. I don't want it to end. Why did you come back down?"

"Brian, I have learned to listen to the voice of God's Spirit. I heard him say "stop" and, as soon as I did, there was an inner knowing of what I needed to do." Sarah opened her briefcase and pulled out a Bible. It was the size of a large paperback book. "I always carry the Word with me. There are times when my spirit craves it, just as the body needs to be fed, the Scripture is food for my soul. I try not to go more than a day or two without reading and meditating on it. I am happy to give this to you. I can get another one, but you need to have this now. I've marked it up a little; maybe those verses I underlined will speak to you as they have to me. God will direct you what to read, but I need go."

She gave Brian a hug and disappeared a second time up the well. Brian looked at the Bible and flipped through the pages. The last time he held a Bible was in high school, probably in youth group and never paid much attention to it. This time he held it with both hands like it was treasure. Even just flipping the pages and feeling the air brush his face seemed to stir his spirit and couldn't wait to start reading. As Sarah left, she advised him to start in the Gospel of John. That's what he would do… later. There was something else to do now... and continued his descent into the well. At the bottom was a platform that crossed to the other side. One could kneel and scoop up the water from the middle of the platform.

Then he heard it. *"Drink deep."* Was this the same voice that Sarah heard? It wasn't audible but somehow, he heard it in his soul. Brian was excited–this was all so new. It was like embarking on a great new adventure and reminded him of an adrenaline rush but different, it was in the spirit rather than at the controls of an F-16. There were paper cups placed on the sides of the platform so people could drink the water. With a cup in hand, he kneeled and filled it with pure clean water and drank slowly savoring the taste as if it was straight from heaven. Then he heard the voice again, *"The water is my Word, drink deep."* That was when it hit. Finishing the cup, he started shaking and couldn't control the praise that was coming out of his mouth. As if flooding his soul, all he could say was "Thank you Jesus, praise you Jesus" repeatedly until it subsided after a couple minutes. When it ended, he was out of breath; it was like a huge static charge had been released and felt depleted but somehow warm and filled with a sense of exhilarating joy and complete peace. He kneeled motionless on the platform for several minutes basking in the divine love flooding his soul.

Brian decided to keep the cup as a reminder of what happened. Standing up on the platform in the center of the well and he turned his eyes straight up. From 200 feet down, he peered through the dimly lit shaft, illuminated by the brilliant sunlit sky at the top. It was like looking through a telescope straight into the light of glory. He ascended the stairs as a different person, totally transformed. Just like the well, sometimes you must go down before you can go up. Brian had drunk from the well of salvation and started humming "Amazing Grace," the only hymn he knew by heart. What he didn't know was that his personal journey of amazing grace was just beginning—the "glory days" he longed for were ahead, not behind.

Chapter 6:

The Chalice

Brian emerged from the well a changed man. Holding a paper cup in one hand and a Bible in the other, both had now become treasures. Seeing a bench near the well entrance, he sat down and examined the street map. After a few minutes, he turned to view the beauty around him. Behind the bench and beyond the railing was a steep bluff descending to the lush green valley below dotted with farms and vineyards as far as the eye could see. Beholding the panoramic view of southern Italy, for the first time in his life, genuine praise filled his soul for the God of all creation.

His thoughts turned to Maryanne and how much he loved her. The encounter in the well seemed to intensify that love. Doesn't the Bible say, *God is love?* Brian thought. Is this what it means? Their tenth anniversary was coming up soon and he had to make it special.

Is there a jewelry store nearby? Maybe he could find something nice here in Orvieto. Plotting a course through the narrow streets, he was once again taken with the charm of this medieval wonderland. A bookstore caught his eye and decided on a slight detour.

What was so special about the well? Emanuella, Maria and the woman at the Papal Palace all seemed to know about it. Is there more to know about Orvieto? Scanning a book on the city's history, he read that Saint Thomas Aquinas taught in Orvieto for several years and wrote many of his early theological treatises. Saint Thomas was considered by the Catholic Church to be the most important philosopher after Aristotle and the Church's greatest theologian. He lived from 1225 to 1274. *Maybe Aquinas played a part of what is going on here.* Brian thought. He bought a few books and set out to find a jewelry store.

There were several shops to choose from, but he was drawn to a store called Pacella's Fine Jewelry and Gifts. Crossing the threshold, Brian noticed a variety of ornate cups, goblets, plates, utensils and more. The craftsmanship was beautiful and forgot all about the jewelry. Walking deeper into the store, one item in particular caught his eye. Behind a locked glass case was a beautiful chalice. There were numerous phrases engraved in what appeared to be an ancient language. What made this chalice so special?

He looked down at the paper cup still in hand. What happened as he drank the water was priceless. The cup needed a container worthy of the experience. Looking closer at the chalice, it was about ten inches high. The base was black marble; the thick stem was made of a dark textured wood carved in a swirl from the base up to the shimmering cup. The cup itself was made of fine gold and was large enough to hold his treasured paper cup from the well.

Approaching the man behind the counter, Brian started asking questions. "Do you speak English?" This always seems to be his opening line here in Italy.

"Yes, a little."

"Can you tell me about the chalice?"

The man's eyebrows rose. "You are interested in the chalice?" He seemed almost incredulous.

"Yes, what can you tell me about it?"

Through a thick Italian accent, he told Brian it was an exact replica of a chalice crafted under strict instructions from Saint Thomas when he lived here in Orvieto. The replica was made by an old jeweler who passed away several years ago. To the man's knowledge, this was the last one. He found it hidden away in a storeroom and placed it on display only last week.

The chalice as a liturgical implement held special meaning, especially for Catholics. During the time of Aquinas, the Church was establishing as Catholic doctrine the belief in *transubstantiation*, which means that, upon the prayer of consecration offered by the priest, the Communion wine in essence becomes the blood of Christ.

This was no ordinary cup! Brian returned to the display case. It was beautiful. "May I see it?"

"Yes, of course," he replied.

The man quickly came around from behind the counter to the display; he fumbled for the right key, opened the case and carefully presented the chalice to Brian using both hands. Taking the chalice from the man's hands, it happened again. He had a sense—a kind of knowing. The chalice was heavy; it must have weighed several pounds. Most of the weight was from the marble base. The wooden stem couldn't have weighed much and then there was the cup at the top made of 24 carat gold. This was going to be expensive. Still, he couldn't shake the sense he was feeling. The chalice was a key to something Brian was meant to discover.

It was odd to find a chalice made of three different materials. The engineer in Brian was intrigued by how they were connected... an old bolt through the base into the thick wooden stem and then threaded into a flange at the bottom of the gold cup allowing a secure fit on both ends with no chance of anything leaking out.

"How much is this?"

"Eight thousand Euros. It is probably worth more. I would rather keep it, but I need the money to stock more popular items." He said through broken English.

Brian didn't know if he was saying that to justify the price… he did some quick math; it was over ten thousand dollars! Oh boy, he will have some explaining to do to Maryanne. She's going to think he went nuts. And he still didn't have anything for their anniversary yet.

Brian's sense of destiny became stronger, as if there was an urgent purpose for him to possess this chalice and comprehend its meaning hidden in some obscure language. There were numerous etchings that appeared to be cryptic phrases. There were four on the base and one that wound around the wooden stem. Looking into the cup, the circular rim was laid out like a compass with the equivalent of the cardinal directions, N-E-S-W, etched on the inside. Opposite each point of the compass, on the outside of the cup was a prominent etching. These four were the most prominent. There was also an inscription inside the cup etched in a circle. *How did he do that?* Brian wondered. Under the base was yet another inscription. It was too mysterious for Brian to pass up. He had read just a little about Saint Thomas and knew he was a spiritual giant. Brian was thirsting to know what truths would be unlocked by these words.

Suddenly, he was racked by fear and doubt. *What am I doing?!* His thoughts mocked him and was about to put it down and walk away when Sarah came to mind. He remembered what she said about being obedient to the voice of God as he tightly held the proof of her obedience in his hand, her own personal Bible. *Was this the voice of God?* he questioned. As he started to put the chalice back in the case, his hands began to tremble. A battle had broken out. A war was raging between his rational mind and his newly activated spirit. Having been in the military, he learned to follow orders, even if you don't understand them. Brian decided to obey the Spirit.

"I will take it under one condition. How can I get these inscriptions translated?"

"The language is not Latin and is very ancient, probably Aramaic. There are only a few scholars that can translate it. My father knew all the meanings, but he passed away many years ago and never told me what they meant. There is an old Jesuit priest in Rome who could help you. I can give you his name; that's all I have."

Brian produced his Delta American Express card. Brian placed the paper cup inside the chalice for safekeeping, and that was where it was going to stay. The shopkeeper wrapped the chalice with great care. For Brian, it would always be a reminder of when he drank from the well of living water at the bottom of a double helix staircase, a symbol that represents the molecule of life itself.

Chapter 7:

The Old Priest

Brian's attention snapped back to the present. It was early afternoon. The day had been a whirlwind so far. Already, so much had happened, but half the day was left. The desire for more sightseeing was gone; his life had suddenly become a quest. With his mind reeling, there was so much to learn. Holding a carefully wrapped chalice in one hand and Sarah's Bible in the other, he did not yet know or understand the powerful symbolism of this picture… but he would in time.

Finding Maria's travel agency on the map, he desperately needed her assistance. Maria saw Brian coming up the steps through the window in her office which was on the ground floor of an ancient brownstone three-story building, like most other storefronts in town. "You must need some help," she said with a smile, coming to the door to meet him. Brian was startled that she was already there waiting for him.

"Yes, I sure do."

"How has your day been so far?" she asked with hopeful expectancy.

"The Duomo was spectacular, just like you said. It was so intense; you can only take so much at once. I wish there was time to carefully look at each sculpture or mosaic before moving to the next. I was only inside for 20 minutes. The Palace was interesting, and I learned a lot by reading the panels... but the well! You must tell me more about the well!"

"Did something happen?"

"When we talked this morning, did you know something would happen?" Brian asked curiously.

"Let's just say, a few people have encountered something spiritual in the well. To be honest with you, most people don't. I don't know what the common denominator is for those who do. What did you experience?"

Brian wasn't sure how much he could tell Maria. "I don't know how you feel about such things. I can tell you this; for some reason, God was in the well. He even arranged for me to have a spiritual tour guide from Texas." He laughed and showed Maria the Bible Sarah had given him. "Can you believe it? She was so knowledgeable about the Word. What are the odds? The whole thing seems orchestrated from above. It makes me feel God has something for me to do. Right now, I have no idea what that may be, but it's exciting!"

Maria was smiling; she had a sense of what Brian had experienced. "God met me and my cousin in the well many years ago. It's why I chose to work in tourism and hope that by promoting Orvieto to America and the world, more people will come and maybe have their own experience. But you came to find me for a reason. How can I help you?"

Brian carefully unwrapped the chalice and placed it on her desk. It was beautiful. With the light shining through the window the golden cup glowed with a rich luster. Maria was in awe–she had never seen it before. "Where did you find this?"

"Ever since the well, it's as if I'm being gently guided. I get a strong sense in my spirit about things. For some reason I was led to Pacella's." he replied.

Then she remembered. She had heard about Pacella's father and the old craftsman who made replicas of Saint Thomas' chalice. But they both died at least twenty years ago. How could there be another one of these replicas still around? She carefully picked it up. It was heavy. "This must have cost a fortune."

"Yes, it did but I felt compelled." *It's a good thing a pay raise came with my bump up to flying international*, Brian thought.

"Why do you have a paper cup inside the chalice?"

"I went to the bottom of the well and was kneeling on the platform with the cup in my hand and I heard a voice in my spirit say, '***Drink deep.***' I can't explain it; I just know that

I heard it. I filled the cup and drank it. Then I heard the voice again in my spirit, *'The water is my Word.'* Sarah had just given me her Bible! At the last drop I was overcome with a sense of joy that can't be explained. It was amazing. It is hard to believe but I know it all really happened. Sarah's Bible and the cup will forever remind me of that moment. To be honest, I bought the chalice as a suitable implement to protect and preserve this ten-cent cup!"

Maria was smiling and nodding as Brian told his story. It wasn't exactly her story. Everyone has a different encounter. She had grown up Catholic but knew that the knowledge of God through his Son was not limited to one brand. Many Catholics would disagree, but Maria was not a legalist in these matters. What about the thief on the cross next to Jesus? He said to him; *Remember me when you come into your kingdom.* Jesus responded and said, *this day you will be with me in paradise* (Luke 23:43). He wasn't Catholic! He wasn't baptized; he didn't go to Catechism or Confirmation. Maria grew up in a Catholic country and knew how religion could become so corrupted with politics. No wonder Martin Luther demanded reform! Being involved with tourism, she had met many fine Protestants who were sincere and committed believers. *They believed in the same God and the same Savior. Did their faith not count just because they weren't Catholic? That doesn't seem possible.* Maria thought.

"My experience was different from yours, but just as impactful." Maria explained. "Since I live here, I want others to know about this place and especially the well. I quit my job with the government to start this travel agency. You too will find yourself drawn to fulfill a purpose."

"I already feel it. It's a sense of being led, but to where? That is another question." Brian responded.

"You will know in time. Now, how can I help you with this chalice?"

"Based on everything else that has happened today, I know there is a reason why we connected at the train station. I need to have these inscriptions translated. Pacella's son, I guess that makes him Pacella Junior, gave me the name of an old priest in Rome who knows ancient languages. He said the inscriptions are not Latin; they may be Aramaic. I need your help to talk with him. If he doesn't speak English, I will never be able to communicate. I thought you might be able to help," Brian said with a pleading smile.

In the few hours after meeting Brian for coffee, Maria was able to take care of the most pressing issues waiting on her desk. The word "purpose" kept coming to mind. *Was there a greater purpose in all this?* she wondered. She could kindly send him away, allowing her to focus on the minutia of the day, or should she risk a little time for the possibility of participating in a plan of higher purpose? She too had learned to obey the voice of the Spirit.

"Brian, let me make a few calls and see where this priest is; maybe he can see us later today."

"Thanks so much, Maria!" Brian sat down in her office and started reading one of his new books on the history of Orvieto.

While Maria began dialing numbers in search of Father Vittorio Gabelli, Brian was searching history looking for any clue that would shed light on the well or the chalice.

There was a section on Saint Thomas of Aquinas, who was called the "Angelic and Universal Doctor of the Church." *What a title!* Brian thought. With a degree in engineering, Brian liked things that were logical. Aquinas made rational arguments for the existence of God and attempted to create a synthesis between Christianity and Aristotle, the founder of the scientific method. Aquinas argued that certain things about God could be known through observation and reason–the first law of the scientific method. This also correlated with the Apostle Paul's argument that God is evident through creation, thereby offering no excuse for atheism.

Aquinas argued that truth enters through two doors. Reason or natural revelation is the first door. This is observation and rational thought. The second door is faith, i.e.

supernatural or spiritual revelation. This is where Aquinas built upon the work of Aristotle and created a synthesis satisfying to Christianity. Supernatural revelation is derived through the inspiration of the Holy Spirit and is communicated to man through the teaching of the Prophets and the Apostles as written and revealed in the Holy Scriptures. It is transmitted from one generation to the next through the authority of the Church. The totality of this revelation is what Aquinas called, "Tradition." Natural revelation is the truth available to all people through their human nature; all men can perceive certain truths from correct human reasoning, such as the existence of a Creator as revealed through His creation.

Brian pondered this for a minute. He liked the argument. He never could get his head around Charles Darwin and his theory of evolution. Even though they tried to shove it down his throat in biology class, it just seemed so inadequate that randomness and chance could account for all the apparent complexity and inherent design seen in all of nature and the universe. He never questioned the existence of God and considered all the so-called proofs of evolution as man's attempt to justify unbelief. As an engineer by training, Brian was very pragmatic. When you see design, you can bet there is a designer somewhere. If every life form on the planet evolved from a single common ancestor, where were all the transitional fossils? There should be millions of them, yet they don't appear to exist. He never bought into evolution; it all seemed too contrived.

While Maria continued her efforts to find the mysterious and apparently elusive Father Gabelli, Brian continued reading about Aquinas and was getting a glimpse of what had happened to him earlier in the well. Though one may deduce the existence of God and some of his attributes through reason, certain specifics may be known only through special revelation found in Scripture such as the trinity, the incarnation, the virgin birth, the sin nature and the need for forgiveness offered to man through Christ. Most theological truths could never be deduced through human reason or natural revelation alone. If they could, then the Apostles would not have had to evangelize the world and die as martyrs for what they believed. Supernatural (faith) and natural revelation (reason) are complementary rather than contradictory. Together they offer a unity of truth; one is natural, and the other is spiritual.

Brian realized what had happened in the well. Through natural revelation, he knew there was a God, that we are not just a random outcome of a billion perfectly timed accidents of chance. His experience was a supernatural revelation of Jesus Christ. This revelation was communicated to him by Sarah and her knowledge of the Scriptures, but it was administered to him through the work of the Holy Spirit. Brian was about to jump out of his seat. *This is great stuff!* his thoughts shouted.

Brian longed to find a connection. Why was this well a place of spiritual encounter? Was it a connection to the Pope? Outside of Rome, only two other Italian cities boasted a Papal Palace–Orvieto and Viterbo. Pope Adrian IV, who reigned from 1154 to 1159, was the first one to spend any time in Orvieto. In 1227, Pope Gregory IX established the Dominican School of Theology called Stadium Generale in Orvieto, one of the first such schools in Europe. Later Pope Urban IV would establish his headquarters in Orvieto. Perhaps because he was French, he never visited Rome! His short reign only lasted from 1261 to 1264, the same time Thomas was in Orvieto teaching at the Stadium Generale. Pope Urban IV had previously been the Patriarch of Jerusalem. Was it a Jerusalem connection?

There had to be a reason why the well was named after St. Patrick. Brian surmised it had nothing to do with its similarity to a cave on Station Island. It must relate to the spiritual encounters attributed to that special cave. Why was it happening here and now in Orvieto? How did the chalice fit into it? Brian sensed the connection was with Saint Thomas and perhaps Pope Urban IV. Did they pronounce a special blessing on Orvieto? They were both Dominicans, which meant "Order of Preachers." According to the Dominican constitution, "The order was instituted principally for preaching and for the salvation of souls."

That's it! Brian thought. That is what happened to him. He didn't just have some spiritual experience; his soul was saved with the help of a Spirit-filled believer from Texas. She wasn't Catholic either. He was getting a sense that this was more than a Catholic thing. It must be a Holy Spirit thing. It didn't happen in the Cathedral or in the Palace, but at the bottom of a well after drinking the purest water he had ever tasted, when physical water became living water. It is the story of Jesus turning water into wine. It is the message of transformation. Brian was ecstatic over this revelation. He had been transformed and understood what happened in his soul was a true miracle; a metamorphosis that could only be accomplished by coming to Christ and being filled with His Spirit.

Brian pondered this for a minute to let it all sink in. Suddenly Maria blurted…

"I got him!" she whispered loudly, covering the mouthpiece. "He is staying at the Three Fountains Abbey in Rome, and he can see us today! He is very intrigued about the chalice and wants to know more, but I told him he had to see it."

"Fantastic!" Brian was excited. It seemed every minute brought a new twist in the adventure. He couldn't wait to unlock the mystery of the chalice. "Can you leave now?" he asked Maria.

Maria paused to think about the demands of the day and then shrugged. "Okay, I just need to tell my assistant where I am going." she said with a quick smile.

A few minutes later they were walking fast toward the taxi stand where they were dropped off that morning. He hated to leave Orvieto, but knew this enchanted place was a portal through time past and its mystique would beckon him back again.

Twenty minutes later they were at the station with no time to spare. As they exited the taxi, the train was pulling into the station from Florence. Brian quickly handed 15 Euros to the cab driver. Brian and Maria ran up the platform and through the doors of the train as they were closing. They would pay for the trip when the ticket-taker came through.

Winded from the run, "I think we're on a whirlwind!" Brian said while claiming a window seat. Maria nodded, catching her breath.

"What all did the priest say when you talked to him?" Brian asked.

"He seemed really surprised that one of the replicas could still be found. Apparently, the craftsman who created them only made a few and thought he could account for all of them. I don't think he believed me at first until I started describing it with all the inscriptions. This priest knows more than what Pacella's son indicated. He must have been acquainted with his father or the craftsman. He knew a lot about this chalice."

"Sounds like we have the right man to help solve this mystery!" Brian exclaimed.

The rolling green Italian countryside raced by as Brian admired the train. It was smooth as butter and amazingly quiet. The sound of the tracks was muted, but he could tell they were traveling well over 100 mph. As a pilot, he liked speed. A good bottle of wine would be nice too. All the vineyards and wineries passing by were putting him in the mood. Sometime that night, a glass of fine Italian wine would be sipped and savored. The FAA required a minimum of eight hours between the last drink and check in. He wished Maryanne could be here to share it with him. *Oh great!* Brian thought. He still didn't have anything for their anniversary. Maybe there would be a jewelry store near the hotel; it would not be pretty to come home empty-handed from his first trip to Italy.

He learned a lot about Maria during the hour-long train ride back to Rome. She grew up in Umbria, which is the province where Orvieto is located. Growing up, her family owned a small farm and grew mostly vegetables, but they were locally famous for their tomatoes. She had four brothers and two sisters. Sadly, only one brother stayed back to run the farm. Maria later moved to Orvieto. All the rest of the kids moved into Rome. Her uncle owned a grocery store, so between the farm and the store, Maria worked from the time she was fourteen. Work is what you do. It is part of the fabric of life, especially in agriculture. She went to college in nearby Perugia, but didn't finish until she was in her late twenties... very typical for Italians. In fact, she didn't move out of her parent's house until she was twenty-nine... also very typical. What's the rush? With a degree in business and a minor in history, her first job was in the local tax assessor's office, but after her own encounter in the well, it was time for a change. Her dad, Mario, provided the seed money to start a travel agency. The whole family remains close. Everyone gets together several times a year when food, wine, laughter, and conversation flow endlessly into the night.

Brian was absorbing Maria's description of life growing up in Italy. It sounded so earthy and more connected to family and the values that make life worth living. Italians in general don't really get started in their careers until their early thirties and even forties. Living life is what they do. A career will happen when they are ready or when necessity dictates.

As Rome got closer, Father Vittorio Gabelli was waiting for them anxiously at Three Fountains Abbey where he lived and studied. As a teacher of Old and New Testament theology for nearly fifty years, his reputation as a scholar was without dispute

Brian looked up the Abbey in the Rome tour guide and was astonished. The monastery was built in the fifth century! Attached to the monastery were three sanctuaries all built in different centuries. The first sanctuary is the oldest and is called Three Fountains. It was built over the site where the Apostle Paul was held in prison and ultimately beheaded. Legend says that when his head was severed, it bounced three times, and a fountain sprang up from all three spots. Not likely, but that was a time when the Apostles were larger than life, like modern day superheroes, and much mythology arose describing their miracles, feats of bravery, and ultimate martyrdom. Brian was excited to see this place. For revenue, the monks grew eucalyptus trees and produced herbal remedies, liqueurs, chocolates and even brewed their own beer. Brian was hoping for a gift shop; Maryanne loves chocolate.

The train was pulling into the station. Thank God for Maria and her fluent Italian. They hopped in a taxi and gave the driver their destination. Brian was a little confused. He had read that this monastery was of the Trappist order and was totally devoted to meditation and prayer as established by Saint Benedict in the sixth century. They had strict codes of silence. *It's not a life I could lead*, he thought. But why was Father Gabelli here? From what Maria said, he was a Jesuit, a teacher and a voracious reader of ancient writings. A Trappist monastery wouldn't seem to be his style. It was a question he would have Maria ask of him.

They exited the taxi and made their way toward the monastery. The grounds were beautiful. The landscaping looked like it was tended every day. Gorgeous eucalyptus trees cast their welcome shade in numerous groves. The manicured grass made him dream of lying down and feeling the earth. A pond was nearby with two elegant white swans gently making their way across the water. This was how he felt in Orvieto; so peaceful it sucked the stress right out of him. He wanted to exhale all the strife and anxiety that comes with living in the modern age and inhale the tranquility that permeated this place. He was beginning to see why Father Gabelli stayed here.

The monastery was built in a quad with four separate wings all connected like a giant square. Each side consisted of a long outside corridor constructed out of stone and was essentially one long covered archway, at least two hundred feet in length. In the center of the quad was a beautiful courtyard with a large flowing fountain in the center. Facing the monastery, along the right side was the interior where the monks lived, studied and prayed. The oldest of the three sanctuaries where the monks would gather for chants and prayers was the one built over Saint Paul's jail and was across the courtyard from where they were walking. In the right-hand corner of the quad was the office for visitors to check-in.

Father Gabelli was waiting for them and rose from an ancient wooden chair as they entered. Looking to be about 80 years old, he was a small man and somewhat hunched over, which made him appear even smaller. His hair was grey, but his eyes were bright blue. Despite his age, he looked sharp and alert. "Buon giorno!" he greeted them in Italian. Maria took the lead.

"It is so good to meet you, Father Gabelli." Maria replied in Italian. "This is Brian Michaels, but he doesn't know Italian. I came along to translate for him."

Father Gabelli looked at Maria with an expression that said, "You underestimate me!" He turned to look at Brian.

"That will not be necessary; I am fluent in many languages, including yours." He said in near perfect English with only a slight accent.

Maria looked a little embarrassed for not asking him on the phone whether he spoke any English. Oh well, she was glad to be there anyway. *There must be a purpose,* she thought.

Chapter 8:

The Quest Begins

They followed the priest back to a small office overlooking the fountain courtyard. Brian quietly ventured a question as they were walking, "Father Gabelli... just curious... I understand you are a Jesuit, so, why are you here in a Trappist monastery?" Brian had read that the Jesuits are a comparatively new order within the timeline of the Church founded by Saint Ignatius of Loyola in 1534, largely as a response to the Protestant Reformation sweeping Europe at the time. The term "Jesuit" means Friends of Jesus or Society of Jesus. As the largest order within the Catholic Church today, with over 18,000 members, they are particularly focused on higher learning and teaching. It seemed odd that a Jesuit would be living within a Trappist order devoted to silence and prayer.

Their shoes echoed against the walls as they made their way to his office. The priest responded in a whisper. "Well to be honest with you, the Monsignor here is a friend of mine from long ago. I don't conduct my teaching here, but I can't think of a better place to absorb myself in study and research. The vow of silence works wonders to center the mind for the task at hand. As long as I don't disrupt the monks, they are pleased to have me."

They arrived at his office and saw the walls were covered with multiple shelves of ancient books. Not a bare wall was visible except above the door. Even below the window, books were stacked up to the bottom of the sill. The priest had his desk positioned to overlook the courtyard with his back towards the door. Situated in front of the desk were two small wooden chairs. He motioned for them to take a seat. The priest closed the door and locked it. The sound of the tumbler mechanism echoed in the hall. Brian and Maria looked at each other. *What was that about?* Walking by his guests, the priest angled the blinds just enough for only light to peer in.

Father Gabelli sat back down with a sigh and a moan from old age and faced his guests. "I am eager to see what you described to me over the phone, Maria." Brian took the package out of a small shopping bag, unwrapped it and placed the chalice on the desk while removing the paper cup and placing it back into the bag. The priest's mouth gaped open. He had seen a few replicas before, but none this beautiful. He picked it up; the others were never this heavy. He 'pinged' the cup with his finger and knew it was pure gold by the dull thud it made. All the other replicas he had seen were only gold plated and would have made a ringing sound.

81

"Where did you find this?" he asked incredulously.

"It was in a display case at Pacella's, a fine gift and jewelry store in Orvieto," replied Brian. "The owner said it was the last replica made by the craftsman who made them, but he didn't know the meaning of the inscriptions. His father knew, Pacella senior, but he died many years ago, before he could tell anyone." Brian thought about what he just said. Perhaps no one was interested! How much knowledge goes to the grave never to be passed on? The treasure of parents so often becomes irrelevant to their children. Only when it is too late is it realized what has been lost.

The priest started to talk. "I have read much about this chalice and have seen replicas before but never anything like this. I honestly don't know where this came from, but it is a genuine masterpiece. It must be very close to the original for the craftsman to use pure gold. The marble is of exceptional quality and the wood comes from the olive tree. I can only assume, based on the overall quality of the chalice, the wood for the stem must be from the Holyland."

He began to look at the inscriptions. "The words are definitely Aramaic, which is unusual; all the replicas I have seen have been in Latin." The priest seemed increasingly mystified and explained how Aramaic is a Semitic language with a 3,000-year history. It was the native language of Jesus and is used today only as part of the liturgy among certain groups of Eastern Rite Christians living in Northern Iraq, Syria and Western Iran. Almost extinct, Aramaic is only used as the primary language in a handful of villages in Syria.

Revealing the Mystery

The Marble Base

- Front Inscription

The old priest got out a pad and pencil and began to translate while seeming to mutter to himself trying to find the English equivalent of what was written in Aramaic. "This is known as *The Chalice of Truth*" he said, pointing to the prominent inscription on the side of the square base.

"Thomas was a master theologian. With this chalice, he crystallized the central truths of the Christian faith through the inscriptions and the materials chosen for crafting it. Do you know why the chalice is made of these specific materials– black marble, wood, and gold?"

Brian and Maria looked at each other shaking their heads. "No, I haven't given it any thought." Brian retrieved a notebook and a pen Maria provided back at her office and began to take notes.

"The marble as rock represents the earth; the blackness of its color is the stain of sin that permeates mankind and the outer darkness where sinners will be cast if they don't repent." Brian winced. That was not something you hear every day. *Outer darkness?* This could get heavy.

The priest continued. "There are ribbons of white throughout the marble which implies that man is capable of doing good things but whatever goodness resides in man is completely overshadowed by our sin nature. The olive wood stem represents the cross of Christ that is planted firmly in the earth and is connected to the golden cup, which represents heaven. Gold always signifies righteousness and purity because it is refined by fire to remove any contamination. The entire Gospel story is told right there. The cross of Christ connects a sinful world to the holiness of heaven."

Brian and Maria sat amazed at hearing his description and he had yet to decipher a single inscription other than the title. "That is really powerful!" responded Brian. "I never realized it, but looking at it now, it makes perfect sense. The chalice was crafted to be a visual metaphor!"

The priest smiled and was glad that Brian was so intrigued.

"Yes, that is true, but it is far more than visual. The inscriptions are the key to unlocking the deepest truths of

God's plan of redemption for a lost and fallen race. I have devoted much study to the chalice. I have just never seen it in Aramaic before and must make sure it is the same as the Latin."

Brian and Maria braced themselves for what was coming. They already knew Father Gabelli was not going to moderate the message to placate any watered-down secular sensibilities. He was a no-nonsense priest and *that* was plainly evident.

- Right Side Base Inscription

He continued writing—and was studying the right side of the base as he wrote. Muttering to himself, he finally spoke. ***Seek truth and live. Seek not and perish***. The priest began to elaborate. "This inscription is parallel with the overall message of the chalice. The *truth* is man's need for forgiveness because of sin. That forgiveness is offered through Christ, but many will not seek it. They will remain in the blackness of sin represented by the black marble. The cross allows them to ascend to heaven as their sins are placed on Christ by faith. So not only does the gold cup represent heaven, but it also represents the righteousness of Christ offered to every believer.

"The inscription emphasizes the duality of our existence and is very blunt and to the point. Aquinas and others in the medieval era did not mince words. Truth is truth, and that truth is Christ. In Christ is life, a life outside of Christ is death. Today we try to accommodate other views; we prefer to think that between black and white there are numerous shades of gray. Is that true? Are there shades of life? I may be old, but I am still alive. Are there shades of death? No, there is no ambiguity; you are either alive or dead. Have you encountered death, perhaps a relative or a friend or maybe a pet? Have you touched their lifeless body? There is a finality of death that is frightening. There are no shades of death and there are no shades of this truth. The modern mind cannot accept it, yet it is exactly what Scripture teaches."

Brian was riveted. Yesterday he probably would have dismissed all this as mumbo jumbo, but today his spirit was eagerly absorbing every word. They were only getting started. Brian knew this mysterious chalice contained a powerful message. Its secrets, hidden in an obscure language, were being revealed one by one by this amazing Jesuit priest. And look where they were! Only yards away from where Saint Paul was martyred for his faith. It all seemed so incredible. Was it just a fantasy? A few hours ago, he was simply a tourist.

- Back Side Base Inscription

The back of the base was next. *Seek knowledge for your mind, Christ for your soul, love for your spirit*. The priest began to explain. "This is how you can know this really comes from the mind of Aquinas. He was a big proponent of using the rational mind for understanding natural truth as Aristotle taught, but he also knew there was a spiritual dimension to man that requires revelation of a supernatural order–revelation that can only be known through Christ and the Spirit of God. It also speaks to the Trinitarian nature of both man and God. Aquinas was a fierce defender of the Trinity as a key doctrine at a time when many core beliefs were under attack by heretical movements regarding the nature of man or the nature of God."

Brian was glad he took the time at Maria's office to read up on Aquinas or this would have been totally over his head. He was both surprised and happy to understand what the priest was talking about. Father Gabelli continued. "Let's take this further; God expects us to use our minds to think. It is the entry point of knowledge. There is a passage of Scripture that says, *my people perish for lack of knowledge* (Hos 4:6).

"However, a relationship with Christ is necessary for the soul. A soul without Christ is lost. Jesus said, *for what shall it profit a man to gain the whole world and lose his own soul* (Mark 8:36).

"Regarding the last part of the inscription, 'Love for your spirit,' the Scripture says, *God is love* (1Jn 4:16), and another verse says, *God is spirit* (John 4:24). Therefore, if the

87

Spirit of God dwells within us, then so does the love of God. For us to *walk in the Spirit* as Paul writes in Galatians (5:25), we must be also walk in love." The priest then added, "Paul also tells us in Romans (5:5) that *God's love has been poured out into our hearts through the Holy Spirit, who has been given to us.*"

Brian took a minute to digest it. *To walk in the Spirit is to walk in love* is what Father Gabelli just said. It must be true! Ever since the well, his heart had been bursting with love. A love he never knew before, a love for God, a love for people, and even a renewed love for Maryanne and Hyler. He always loved them, but now it was different, it was more intense; somehow it had a spiritual dimension. He looked at Maria sitting next to him and then thought of Sarah. He loved these women, but not in some sexual or perverse way; it was a love that was pure and clean. Brian shook his head as he acknowledged this revelation and tried to focus again on what the priest was saying.

- Left Side Base Inscription

The left side of the base was next. It was a verse right out of the Bible based on something Jesus said: *Ask and it shall be given; seek and you shall find; knock and it shall be opened*. (Luke 11:9) The priest again elaborated. "This inscription has to do with prayer, how we communicate with our Heavenly Father. Notice the first word is "ask." There is a verse that says, *we have not because we ask not* (James 4:2). If you have a need in your life, don't be afraid to ask. He wants you to come to him like a child would come to a loving parent for an answer. The next word is "seek." Hebrews 11:6 says *God is the rewarder of those who diligently seek him.* This is so important. People barely make any attempt to seek God and then wonder why he seems so distant. God hides himself expressly for those who are willing to seek him. When we do seek him, we are rewarded with a new revelation, a nugget of truth or maybe an answer to prayer. The last word is "knock." I think this is best understood as the way God guides us in life. As we pray and as we seek, he will open the doors you are meant to go through and close the ones you are not. These are all action verbs meaning we are to keep on asking, keep on seeking and keep on knocking as we go through life. It is how we stay connected with God and stay on course with his will for our lives. Once connected, God will speak to us if we listen for his leading. In fact, scripture teaches that, *whoever is united with the Lord is one with him in spirit* (1 Cor 6:17).

Brian was piecing it all together and thinking about what happened in the well. Once he asked Christ into his life, it was like his spirit was activated, or as the priest said, connected. It was only then that he heard God's voice in his own spirit. Other times that day he felt led or drawn as when he ended up at Pacella's. Brian was in spiritual overdrive. What Father Gabelli was teaching resonated with his own experience and reinforced his assurance that it was real. It was not just his imagination.

- Underside Base Inscription

Father Gabelli continued his examination—looking at the underside of the base. It was another verse from Scripture. *The stone that the builders rejected has become the cornerstone* (Luke 20:17). The priest again explained. "This has both a specific and a general application. Aquinas selected this verse because the marble of the base is essentially stone. However, he introduced a new metaphor–Jesus as the cornerstone of the church. The specific application is that Jesus was talking to the Jews when he said this. Although many Jews accepted him as the Messiah, such as all the Apostles and most of the first century church, a great number of Jews, starting with those in political authority, rejected him. They feared the reaction of Rome and they were afraid for their own positions of power. Jesus was upsetting the applecart. After the resurrection, the Church spread quickly through the teaching of the Apostles. However, Jews were forbidden to follow this new sect and were threatened with expulsion from the synagogue. This was a big deal; all aspects of community life centered around the synagogue. It was like being expelled from the community of all your family and friends. Consequently, most Jews thought the price was too high and instead many joined with groups that were persecuting the fledgling church."

The priest continued. "So, the specific application is that Jesus is the stone rejected by the Jews. What the Jews failed to understand is that, through them, God was launching a plan to bring salvation to the Gentiles based on faith. Judaism as revealed in the Old Testament was a religion based on following rules known as the Law, but the New Testament introduces a whole new covenant. God knew the sin nature was too powerful within us for man to ever measure up to the demands of the Law. Therefore, God fulfilled the Law for us through Christ and now simply asks us to accept him by faith and believe what he has accomplished for us. It truly is marvelous when you think about it. Sadly, not only did the Jews reject this, but the world has also largely rejected Christ. This has been played out in history. The Romans persecuted the Church for the first 300 years until Constantine. In more recent times, ever since the Enlightenment or the Age of Reason of the 1700s, the western world has grown increasingly secular, recklessly abandoning the moral structure of religion as a benefit to society and ignoring their individual need for Christ. A nebulous form of existentialism permeates the modern age, especially in Europe. And people wonder why drug abuse, depression and suicide are at record levels."

Brian and Maria were mesmerized and were doing their best to take it all in. It seemed so natural for Father Gabelli, even effortless, as he explained and expounded on each inscription. He spoke so matter-of-factly about things others would avoid. Brian loved his direct style as opposed to America's preoccupation with political correctness, and what some might call "wokeness." He was receiving pure, undiluted truth and was hanging onto every word. Brian wanted to take a break to digest it all, but knew he was running out of time.

- The Wooden Stem

Next up was the stem made of olive wood. Winding around the stem from the base to the cup was another inscription running up the entire length–about four inches. After the priest finished writing down the translation, he said "Before I tell you what is next, it is important for you to understand something about the base. Except for the verse on the bottom, all the inscriptions are about seeking. The essence is that unless we seek to know God through Christ, we cannot know him. We perhaps can know things about God, but we cannot truly know him. Knowing comes through seeking."

"How does one seek him?" Brian asked.

The old priest peered at Brian with a quizzical look. Brian felt a little sheepish, almost like the priest was saying, *I can't believe you don't know this*. "We can seek him in prayer, through the Scriptures and through the Church," replied Father Gabelli. The Age of Reason discarded any belief in the supernatural, which began our downward path to secularism. Here is where the unbelieving world misses it. The wind is a perfect metaphor; you can't see the wind, but you can see its effect. You can even feel it, but you still can't see it. It is the same with the Spirit. You can feel His presence within, and you can see His effect in people's lives, but you cannot see the Spirit of God directly. It requires faith."

The priest continued. "You see, there was a time when scientists openly acknowledged their faith in God, like Newton, Galileo, Copernicus and Kepler. They could observe the night sky and behold the greatness of the Creator. *Brian could relate to that!* Their faith didn't prevent them from being good scientists. Today, the sciences are consumed with a materialist worldview that says only what can be observed is real. Consequently, they have discarded God. The ancients knew better. This was the genius of Aquinas. He was a theologian, a philosopher and a scientist. He didn't view these disciplines as mutually exclusive. For Aquinas and others, until the Age of Reason, these disciplines worked together to reveal the deep mysteries of an infinite God. Not anymore, the materialists have taken over and, oh, how sad it is."

Brian thought about what the priest said about how science has been overtaken by a materialist view. It is baffling how smart people with doctorate degrees can believe our DNA got packed with 3.3 billion lines of complex genetic information by an unguided random process without any consideration of a divine origin. The blindness of unbelief is truly profound.

Father Gabelli continued with his explanation of the stem. "The inscription is another verse from John's Gospel; *I am the way, the truth and the life* (John 14:6). This is a perfect verse for the stem. The vertical position of the stem points the way to heaven. There is only one stem and there is only one way to God. There are many people in the world that would object, but truth is truth, and it doesn't change just because someone doesn't agree with it. The rest of this verse, if you were to read it in the Bible, says, *"No one comes to the Father but by me."* This statement is even more exclusive. How can this be? Look at the chalice. The black base of our sin nature is connected to a holy God through the cross. Without the cross there is no way the two can meet. They are like the two poles of a magnet that repel each other. Light cannot dwell with darkness and sin cannot dwell with holiness. The cross makes the connection. Many will reject this truth and that is what the inscription on the bottom anticipates; *the stone the builders rejected...* sadly, millions will reject. Although for many, the chief complaint is that Christianity is too exclusive. The irony is that Christ rejects no one who comes to him with humility and repentance. The proud, the arrogant, and the rebellious can never come to Christ without repentance because they demand heaven on their own terms instead of those established by God. It is a sad truth. Just as the gold cup represents holiness and heaven, the black base represents sin and outer darkness. Through an act of our own will, we choose our eternal destination. If only people understood how total forgiveness of sin, no matter what they may have done in the past, has been paid for at the cross and available to them by faith. However, many don't even acknowledge that sin is their problem."

The wise priest continued. "It was sin that broke our relationship with God in the first place. It started in the Garden. It is what prevents humanity from having a relationship with Him now. Jesus came to restore that relationship by taking sin out of the equation. Yet people willfully turn away from the one who accomplished this for them. And then they wonder why God seems so distant. They question his very existence. Their sin nature alienates them from God and ultimately leads them to total rejection. In the darkness of their minds, they run after false religions or devolve into atheism. The answer to their problem stares them in the face every time they see a cross, yet they choose to remain blind to the truth."

This is getting heavier by the minute, Brian thought. He never really considered the consequences of rejecting

Christ. The whole idea of being eternally separated from God in outer darkness sent shivers through his spine. There was so much to think about already. Brian braced himself for the cup.

Chapter 9:

The Cup

Father Vittorio Gabelli, a Jesuit for fifty years and a man of immense wisdom and learning, looked up from his pad. He moved the chalice closer to where Brian and Maria were sitting and leaned back in his chair. They had only been there an hour, but it felt like an eternity as this amazing man of God revealed deep truths hidden in an ancient language. Why was Brian caught up in all this? He wasn't even Catholic. In fact, he came to realize he wasn't really a Christian until today, at the bottom of a 500-year-old well. Who is going to believe this story? It was as if he was caught up in a fable like The Chronicles of Narnia or The Lord of the Rings. It all seemed so surreal.

"You both appear dazed," the priest observed. "Am I going too fast?"

Brian shook his head, but Maria responded, "What you have explained is so powerful, it is hard to take in all at once, but I know we must keep going. Brian flies out tomorrow back to Atlanta and I must return to Orvieto. Please continue."

"I must warn you; the message of the cup is full of wonder and woe. I could use a break myself before revealing the next set of messages, but ... time is pressing."

- The Compass Markers

The priest leaned forward, pulled the chalice closer and looked inside. He angled the chalice toward Brian and Maria so they could see inside. "Notice the four letters inside the cup at the top of the rim. They are aligned with the four corners of the base and represent the four points of the compass. There is a reason for their location at the top of the cup. Only a knowledge of Scripture could reveal what this means. As with the base, the cup represents more than one metaphor."

The priest continued. "This may be difficult to digest but if you are to leave here with understanding, you must know the full meaning of the chalice. There are two applications regarding the inside rim. It represents the end of the age. The compass markers are at the very top of the rim and correspond to the fullness of time. If you can imagine that time is like the sands of an hourglass and the cup represents the total amount of time allotted for man, then the top of the chalice, the rim, would indicate the end of time. In the Apocalypse or what Protestants would call the book of Revelation; four horsemen are released to bring judgment on a world that has rejected Christ. At this same time, God also gathers his elect from the four corners of the earth as indicated by the four points of the compass. This is when Jesus, also called the 'groom,' returns for his Church, known as the 'Bride of Christ.' Scripture tells us the relationship Jesus has with his Church is like the mystical union of a man and wife in marriage, they have become one in spirit. At some point in the near future, the groom will return to retrieve his bride. Protestants often call this the Rapture or the Catching Away. Catholics don't really have an official name for it other than our "gathering together in him." There are many views on the timing of this event so I don't want to debate when it will happen, but we certainly believe it is coming soon."

Brian was taken aback by the priest's end-time references. A few of his Christian friends from the golf club had talked about this in conversation. They mentioned the formation of the state of Israel in 1948, Jewish control of Jerusalem in 1967, and the Russian alliance with Iran as signs of its approach, that these events were fulfillments of biblical prophecy. Others had mentioned Artificial Intelligence and Crypto Currency as moving us closer to a cashless society where the government has total control. Brian was beginning to wonder; *were they right? Could the return of Christ be soon?*

- Inside the Cup

The priest peered into the center of the cup and turned it so he could read the full inscription, which was in the form of a circle. He wrote it down on his pad. "This is another verse of Scripture from John's Gospel, which tells what happened after Christ died on the cross. The Romans needed to make sure Jesus was dead before they could release the body to be buried. So, they took a spear and thrust it into his side, and the Scripture says, *out flowed blood and water* (John 19:34). This is also what the inscription says, and it is very important. The location is perfect."

"I don't get it." Brian chimed in. "Why is the location of that inscription on the inside of the cup so important? Why would it make any difference?"

"Allow me to explain." Father Gabelli smiled with a look of complete knowing. "The order of words is critical. First came blood. This was atoning blood, the blood of the perfect sacrifice so our sins could be forgiven. This was foreshadowed when the Jews were required to kill a lamb and put the blood on the doorposts of their houses in Egypt. Do you remember the story? At the command of God through Moses, ten plagues came against Pharaoh, the king of Egypt, to force his hand in releasing the Jews from slavery. The tenth and final plague resulted in the death of all firstborns, both human and animal. To prevent this calamity from happening to the Jews, they were commanded to put the blood of a spotless lamb on their doorposts. The Angel of Death would see the blood and pass over them. Ever since then, the Jews have celebrated Passover every year; it is the most important day on their calendar.

"In the New Testament, John the Baptist looks at Jesus coming to be baptized in the Jordan River and says, *Behold the Lamb of God who takes away the sins of the world* (John 1:29). Jesus was God's sacrifice, his own sinless son, given for the sake of man. Jesus marked the earth, our house, with his own blood. The Scripture says, *Life is in the blood* (Lev 17:11), it also says, *Without the shedding of blood there is no remission of sins* (Heb 9:22). The shedding of Christ's life-giving blood became the perfect sacrifice required to overcome sin and death. It was a trade made in heaven: he who was sinless took our sins upon himself including the consequent penalty of death in a perfect act of divine love. All God asks us to do is believe.

"But there is more." He continued. "The verse says *out flowed blood and water*. This is what John saw and there are some medical explanations for it, but the spiritual application is what's most important. Water represents the Holy Spirit. This is why the priest, when preparing the wine for the Eucharist or Communion, usually mixes the wine with a little water. It stems from this verse. The application is the key. We cannot receive the Holy Spirit without first applying the blood of sacrifice by asking his forgiveness. It is after our souls have been cleansed of sin by the blood of Christ that the Holy Spirit can fill a person's soul represented by the water.

That certainly explained what happened to me! Brian thought.

Father Gabelli held up the chalice and began to examine the inscriptions on the side of the cup. They were positioned to line up with the compass markers on the inside rim. The inscription began about a half inch below the top and continued down to about a half inch above the bottom. The width of each inscription was about an inch and a half. In between each inscription was etched a thin cross about two inches high and centered in the middle of the cup. He picked up his pencil and began to write.

- North Compass Marker Inscription

Clean the cup, clean your soul. Fill the cup, fill your soul. The priest began his explanation. "This inscription is very interesting, which I will explain, but its position under the North compass marker is curious. The North Star has been a reliable navigation guide for thousands of years. It is positioned as the last star in the handle of the Little Dipper constellation. It is ironic that the Little Dipper is also a cup, the same as this chalice. The Scripture implies that the physical location of heaven is in the northern sky, behind the

North Star. It suggests that heaven is both a spiritual and physical reality.

"The inscription itself relates to the one inside the cup, which is symbolic of your soul. Think about it. We are nothing more than containers. We will be filled with something. Will it be God, or will it be sin and worldliness? We are all born with a sin nature. Inevitably, the longer we live the more sin we collect in our souls. From the worst offender to the near saint, sin taints us. No one escapes it. We are all filled in varying degrees with lust, greed, envy, jealousy, anger, hatred, pride and probably a few more. What does this lead to? It leads to lies, theft, adultery, violence, murder and a host of perversions, addictions and compulsions. A lifetime of filling this cup with sin would look disgusting if you could see it. And yet we DO see it played out in the lives of those taken over by sin. It is a picture of the alcoholic who comes home drunk and beats his wife and kids. It is the man or woman who allows their affections to be drawn to another in lust resulting in divorce and a broken family. It is the man who lashes out with violence out of jealousy or a woman who manipulates and undermines another marriage because of envy. It results in lies to cover up what we know is wrong. It is greed that leads to theft, embezzlement, swindling, cheating and more. It is sexual perversion played out through pornography, pedophilia, incest, bestiality and all other sexual sins.

"This is what is in your cup, and you are totally powerless to clean it. How many New Year's resolutions have you managed to keep? Are you any better at keeping the commandments of God? No. We are powerless to truly live a life free from sin. This is why the sacrifice of Christ is so essential. It is not an option. Jesus did not mince words, he said, *Unless you repent, you too will all perish* (Luke 13:3). Repent means to change your mind, to come to your senses, to alter the direction of your life. Jesus also said, *if you do not believe that I am the one I claim to be, you will indeed die in your sins* (John 8:24). Can you imagine dying with all that filth still in your cup? What chance of heaven would there be? It is ludicrous to think we could be allowed entry into the Kingdom of God, a place of complete holiness, with all that garbage still in our souls. So, the inscription reads; ***Clean the cup, clean your soul***. We clean it by coming to Christ and allowing him to remove our sins from us. His blood has already been offered as a sacrifice and is the only thing that can atone for sin. Jesus then takes our sins and buries them in the ground with his crucified body. Yet, he did not remain in the ground but rose from the dead victorious. Jesus was sinless. Satan had no legal right to kill him. Therefore, God was completely justified to raise him from the dead and restore him to his former glory, the glory he had in heaven before coming to earth as a babe in the manger. God allows us to participate in his death and his resurrection by faith. His death is our death; his resurrection is our resurrection. In everything, Jesus becomes our substitute!"

Brian stood up and walked to the window. "Father Gabelli, this is wonderful. I became a believer, I mean, a true believer, only today. Every word you say is like water pouring onto a dry sponge!" The priest smiled. It is not often that a student will respond with such passion. He was grateful for the opportunity.

Brian sat back down and was shaking his head, trying to wrap his brain around all that was being said. The priest continued. "There is more; once we are made clean through Christ, our cup can be filled with his Holy Spirit, which is crucial if we are to live a life of faith. We cannot do it on our own. This is central to our understanding what salvation really means. The inscription reads; *Fill your cup, fill your soul.* This is the meaning: there is no way God would allow his Spirit to indwell a soul soiled with sin. It would be like taking a filthy cup, filling it with pure clean water and then putting it to your lips to drink. You wouldn't do it. And neither will God fill a dirty vessel with his Spirit. In fact, a dirty cup is useless. Look at your own kitchen. Dirty cups are in the sink; clean ones are in the cabinet. The ones in the sink will not be used again until they are cleaned. You cannot be used either until your soul has been made clean through Christ. To be used by God may be a foreign idea to you, but what is the point of our existence if we have no use to our maker? The first step in being used by God is to be filled with the Holy Spirit. So, put it all together. God made the cup (you). Sin caused the cup to become filthy and unfit for his use. Jesus cleans the cup and makes us ready to be filled with the Holy Spirit! It is a perfect metaphor for the work of the Trinity. Knowing the importance of cleansing and filling is what sets Christianity apart from every other religion or philosophy. It is vital to our understanding if we are to successfully live the abundant life God promised."

Brian and Maria felt like they were drinking from a fire hose. The priest was talking non-stop, and Brian was furiously taking notes... but it all made sense. This explained why he started getting revelation from God after he came to Christ in the well and not before. God may have been prompting him or even leading him, but it was after he came to Christ that he got zapped, so to speak.

Brian kept thinking about the idea of cleansing and filling. It was powerful and answered a lot of questions. It explains why so many Christians appear so lukewarm or come off as hypocrites. Perhaps they were cleansed when they first came to Christ but have done little to keep their cups filled with his Spirit. They have allowed themselves to be filled with sin and worldliness instead. As a result, their faith lacks depth and commitment. Perhaps they are like he was only yesterday, a believer in the concept of God but having no real relationship with Christ.

Brian's mind was reeling with one revelation after another as Father Gabelli unpacked more truth with every word he spoke. He wanted to digest what he already learned, but there was no time. They had to press on.

- East Compass Marker Inscription

The priest was looking at the next inscription under the east compass marker, *Cup of peace, cup of blessing*. He began to explain. "This inscription is under the East symbol for a reason. The east is associated with the sunrise. It speaks of new beginnings and new possibilities. The rising sun points to the Son of God who rose from the darkness of death just as the sun rises from the darkness of night. The sun fills our day with brilliant light and warmth; Jesus fills our souls with the light of his love and the warmth of his Spirit. It speaks of a new day. The prophet Jeremiah writes in Lamentations that *God's mercies are new every morning* (Lam 3:22). It is fitting that the direction of the sunrise represents mercy and blessing. Paul writes in Romans that we have *peace* with God through Christ. He writes in Ephesians that we have been *blessed* with every spiritual blessing in Christ. This is why Paul, in his first letter to the Corinthians, calls the Communion cup itself the *cup of blessing* (1 Cor 10:6). In the most famous of all the Psalms, David writes; *you prepare a table before me in the presence of my enemies, you anoint my head with oil; my cup overflows* (Ps 23:5). That overflowing cup is the cup of peace and blessing, even in the midst of enemies or in the valley of death. At the end of the day, if our life is in Christ, we have nothing to fear, not even death.

Father Gabelli's Jesuit training was in high gear! Brian remembered his church youth leader—a real Bible whiz. If you gave him a verse, he could tell you right where it was. This priest knew the Scriptures inside and out too. It was a natural flow, as if the Scripture was part of the very fabric of his soul. It resonated with Brian because it wasn't filled with pious platitudes or religious dogma—it was pure—as pure as the water at the bottom of St Patrick's Well.

Brian and Maria were both exhausted and overloaded. Their brains could barely absorb any more. Brian looked at his watch. It was late afternoon. He could stay a little longer. He refocused his mind and hoped for a second wind to keep going.

Chapter 10:

A Message of Woe

The priest was tired but had to finish. Revealing the message of the chalice was too important. Who knows where all of this would lead? Father Gabelli also believed in divine purpose; the idea that things happen for a reason. Why should he doubt that God had orchestrated this meeting? He started on the third inscription. He shuddered as he transcribed the message onto his writing pad. Brian sensed something was wrong; he leaned forward. "What does it say? What does it mean?"

- West Compass Marker Inscription

The inscription read, *Cup of judgment, cup of wrath.* "This is the hardest one to reveal." He bowed his head and became quiet. The look on his face was somber and mixed with grief. After a minute, the priest regained his composure and stared at the pad where he had written the translation.

"This is so awful and so sad that I can hardly bear to talk about it, but I must. To not reveal it would be an act of hate as opposed to love. This inscription is positioned under the west compass marker. The west suggests sunset–the end of the day. The sunset points to judgment and impending

109

darkness. The light of day only lasts for a while. Jesus said we are to *work while it is still day, the night is coming when no one can work* (John 9:4). We are allotted a certain number of years to live. What will we do with the time God has given us? The night will finally come with our own death, and it will come for the whole world at the end of the age. I mentioned this when we first started talking about the cup. The four points of the compass also refer to the four horsemen of the Apocalypse and the gathering of the saints from the four corners of the earth. When the sands of time have run out, the cup will be full. So, what happens next?

"God is a righteous judge. He loves mercy. He extends grace to all who ask in humility and sincerity. The cup of judgment can only be poured out by a judge. There is a coming day of judgment for all who have lived and are currently living. The meaning of this inscription is made clear from Scripture. We just talked about the cup as a cup of blessing. A new meaning is introduced with this inscription– **Cup of judgment, cup of wrath.** In both the Old Testament and in the Apocalypse or the book of Revelation, the word "cup" is often used within this context. In the Old Testament, when Israel abandoned God to follow false religions, he viewed it as betrayal and adultery. After many attempts at offering mercy, His judgment eventually fell swiftly and severely. God described this judgment as: *cup of my fury*; *cup of trembling*; and *cup of astonishment and desolation* (Is

51:17, Ez 23:33). God used the enemies of Israel to be the unwitting agents of his punishment.

"In the book of Revelation, God uses similar words to describe what happens to a world that has rejected his Son, thereby rejecting him. Listen to these descriptions–*the cup of his indignation* and *the cup of the wine of the fierceness of his wrath* (Rev 14:10, Rev 16:19). These are not pretty pictures. They reveal a God who is fed up with his own creation rejecting him as their Creator, rejecting his Word, rejecting his moral laws and rejecting his own Son who paid the ultimate price for their redemption. There is a day of reckoning when judgment comes upon the whole world and yet the prophetic signs of his return are continually ignored, just as Israel also ignored the prophets who warned them.

"I grieve for the people who will be lost. In the hardness of their hearts, many will not turn to the God who loves them. There is still time for people to repent and be saved, but that time grows very short. I fear the sand is near the top of the cup with only a few grains left to fall.

"Perhaps that is why you are here, Brian… Maria. Perhaps the message of this chalice, crafted 800 years ago by the Church's greatest theologian, will turn the hearts of people back to the God who made them and loves them."

Brian was silent. He suddenly felt a tremendous burden to share this message with so many friends and relatives who were living apart from Christ. The thought of loved ones cast into outer darkness was horrifying. If only he could share with others his experience today in the well. If only he could tell them what he had learned from Father Gabelli and the message of the chalice. Tears welled up in his own eyes as he was gripped with the consequences of rejecting Christ and how little time remained to tell those he loved. Maria's head was buried in her hands. She too was struck by the awful reality of even one friend or relative lost without hope.

- South Compass Marker Inscription

Brian could hardly take any more. In a hesitant tone he asked, "Father Gabelli, is there still more?"

"Yes, there is one last inscription. It is one of great hope. I have already transcribed it." He looked at his notes. "It is what you might expect to find on a Communion chalice. It reads, *My body broken for you, my blood shed for you, consume my presence*. It is curious that it is set under the South compass marker. Just as North implied heaven, South in this metaphor implies death and hell. That is what awaits those who reject God's perfect sacrifice. God has no choice. God's perfect justice was satisfied through the sacrifice of his only Son. Rejection of that sacrifice leaves no alternative for that person but to receive God's judgment for their own sins... and that judgment is death… eternal separation from God. As I stated earlier, sin cannot dwell in the presence of a Holy God.

"For the believer, Jesus has already died in their place. They have *passed from death to life* (John 5:24) and are delivered from the penalty of hell. This is why we are implored to partake in Communion in remembrance of what he accomplished for us on the cross. He said *do this in remembrance of me* (Lk 22:19). We must be in Christ by faith, and he must be in us by the power of his Spirit. The Eucharist is a physical and visible reminder of the extreme price paid for our salvation. We can never lose sight of this truth. We Catholics believe the bread and wine become the Real Presence of Christ upon consecration by the priest. Brian, I know you are not Catholic, so I don't want to enter a debate about the mystery of the Communion meal. Let me just say this, it is something we should do often and in fellowship with other believers to celebrate the sacrificial love of Christ as we await his return."

Brian was pleased that Father Gabelli embraced Brian's faith as real and authentic; he made no attempt to persuade him that the Catholic way was somehow the only way. His faith transcended the legalism of religion and came through with the force of his words. It was as if Christ was the very essence of his being. It was pure and powerful and gave

113

Brian the assurance that everything he had heard from this wise and remarkable priest was trustworthy and true.

Chapter 11:

Go Ye Therefore

Father Vittorio Gabelli stood up from his desk and walked toward a small cherry wood cabinet in the corner. It was locked. Pulling a key from his pocket, he opened the right-side door. Brian and Maria were both watching as he carefully removed a chalice. It looked just like the one from Orvieto! He placed it on the desk in front of them while they pulled their chairs closer to examine both chalices side-by-side. At first glance, they looked the same, but upon closer inspection, they were quite different. In fact, Brian's was noticeably more authentic... he couldn't exactly tell why, his simply looked... older, much older. The difference between the Latin and Aramaic inscriptions was also apparent.

"Brian, looking at these together, I know what the difference is," said the old priest. He had a distant, pensive look in his eyes. "Somehow, the one you bought must be another chalice crafted by Aquinas himself. I was not aware of there being another one. It may even be the original, because no one knows where it is. You see, the craftsman you mentioned who made this replica was my brother, Giovanni Gabelli. He passed away many years ago and never saw the original chalice. The replicas he made were from sketches and drawings found in a manuscript created by Aquinas with only a few known copies. One is kept in the Papal Palace in Orvieto. This is how Giovanni was able to craft the replicas. But the one you have is different and much older.

"I have come to this conclusion, Brian; Aquinas did not develop the chalice himself but must have obtained the original version from somewhere else. The original, also lost, was probably from the first or second century. It is the only thing that explains the Aramaic. Aquinas must have made a copy of the original, which you have here. He also made a version with inscriptions in Latin so the people of his day could read and comprehend its message. Aquinas most likely added or changed certain inscriptions from the original to reflect his own theology. The chalice sketched in the book found in the Papal Palace reflected only the Latin version. I don't believe anyone ever knew there was an earlier version in Aramaic! Pacella senior, who owned the store in Orvieto, must have obtained this chalice before he died... but from who, when and where is unknown. There is no record of it, nor did he tell anyone. My brother didn't know. He would have told me, and neither did Pacella's son who now runs the shop. He must have discovered it while rummaging through a storeroom and just put it on display thinking it was merely another one of Giovanni's replicas.

"Brian, you have stumbled onto a treasure of immense worth! There is a reason for this to come into your possession. All the truths of the chalice have been revealed to you. Now you must do something with it."

Brian picked up the chalice and held it again, this time regarding it with new understanding and appreciation. As valuable as the chalice was, its message was priceless. He didn't think about the money spent and how it may have been the best investment he ever made. He could never think of selling it. No; the only thought he had at that moment was what to do with it, or, better yet, what God wants him to do with it.

"Father Gabelli, I don't know how to thank you for your time and your wisdom. You have been invaluable to me. Is there something I can do for you?"

The old priest just shook his head. "No, Brian, my needs are simple. You see where I live. The best gift you can give me is to tell the world about the Chalice of Truth and the message it holds for the future. People must know that Jesus is coming back, not as a baby, not as a carpenter, not as a teacher, but as the King of Kings who will judge the world according to his Word, the Holy Scriptures. If we respond to its message, there is mercy; if we reject its message, there is judgment. Tell the people, Brian, tell the world! Time is growing short."

Brian reached into the shopping bag from Pacella's and retrieved the paper cup from the well and carefully put it back inside the chalice, wrapped them together and placed the package back into the bag.

Father Gabelli saw the paper cup but said nothing. He recognized where it came from, and a knowing smile came to his face.

"Is that all you have to carry it?" asked the priest.

"I'm afraid so, it's all I could find." replied Brian.

Father Gabelli reached into a desk drawer and gave Brian a strong canvas bag imprinted with a picture of the monastery. "This is from last year's annual fund raiser. It should fit nicely." Taking his translation notes and putting them in an envelope, he handed them to Brian. "Don't lose these!" he cautioned. After calling a taxi, the priest walked Brian and Maria out to the courtyard and by the time they emerged from the long archway, a cab was waiting for them. The three new friends shook hands, embraced and parted ways.

"Train station, please," Maria told the driver in Italian. "Brian, this may have been the best day of my life. I don't know how to thank you for introducing yourself this morning. I have a feeling you will be coming back to Orvieto, and I certainly look forward to it."

"Maria, I am in a daze. Our paths did not cross by accident. There may be many more people coming to visit Orvieto by the time I'm done. You can be sure I'll be in touch."

The taxi pulled up to the train station. "Maria, can you let the driver know my destination? I'll just stay in this cab." Maria did so. Brian stepped out and gave Maria a hug. She turned and made her way to the platform to wait for the next train to Orvieto. With a last little wave, she disappeared into the crowd.

Back in the car, the taxi moved onto the streets of Rome heading due west. It was early evening and the sun was setting, filling the sky with a vibrant array of colors. As beautiful as it was, he couldn't help but think of the West compass marker on the cup and how time was setting too.

Chapter 12:

Back to Reality

Brian Michaels paid the taxi driver and walked into the hotel lobby holding a canvas bag containing a treasure of infinite value: Sarah Foxworth's Bible, a chalice worth far more than what he paid, and a paper cup worth nothing and worth everything. He was a completely different person from the one that walked out that morning.

Not wanting to return to his tiny room just yet, he sat down in a seating area near the check-in counter. It was a circle of four soft chairs. A TV was on in the background, tuned to BBC International. He couldn't look at it—too much reality too soon. He turned to see if Emanuella was there, but her shift ended two hours ago. An impressionist painting drew his gaze. It pictured an outdoor café and reminded him of meeting Maria that morning for coffee. Would he ever be able to tell Maryanne about Maria without having her reel with jealousy and suspicion? The mindset is common to pilots' wives who constantly worry about husbands far away— staying in hotels with friendly flight attendants only a few doors down. Too many rumors become reality, adding fuel to insecurities. *At least Maria wasn't a flight attendant!* Brian thought. Explaining today was going to be a challenge.

Luckily, no one was sitting near him. Brian was lost in his thoughts. He had never been unfaithful to Maryanne. Sure, the eyes may have strayed from time to time but never acted on any such impulse. He had flown with pilots who made a habit of frequenting the local strip clubs and would join them from time to time—but never told Maryanne. Now… just the thought seemed foreign. *That was a new feeling!* Before, joining in the revelry would have seemed okay as long it was kept just between the boys. He wasn't being unfaithful, not literally. Pondering these thoughts and how his attitudes and desires had changed was a confirmation of what happened this day. He had so many questions about his new faith and was glad to have Sarah's email. *Oh, great!* Brian thought, another woman he would have to explain to Maryanne.

How was it possible to have both a sense of joy and burden at the same time? There was joy for all the experiences the day brought, but also the burden that came from learning, at the feet of an old and wise priest of the mission that lay ahead. He left that morning as a tourist and returned as a soldier with orders from above. Now what? Brian thought about the elements of any mission. It would begin with defining the objective, establishing an achievable goal, moving forward with preparation, developing a plan, executing that plan and, finally, evaluating the results. He shook his head. How did all that apply to what he learned? Brian was overwhelmed and needed someone to help him sort it all out. Unfortunately, that was not going to be Maryanne. In fact, his immediate mission would be to explain everything to her. Would she flip out with anger over the money he spent on the chalice? Would her jealousy ignite over the women who helped him?

Brian stood up. It was time to put his things away and find a store before everything closed... plus, he was starving having only eaten a pastry for breakfast and no lunch. He took the elevator to the fourth floor and found his room just as it was earlier. There was a safe in the closet; putting the canvas bag in and pulling the key out, he was ready to go.

As Brian exited the elevator, Tom Jennings and two of the flight attendants, Jenny and Suzanne walked into the lobby. They all had a few drinks, and he could tell they were loosened up. "Hey Brian," Tom called out. "Where have you been all day?"

"You got my voice mail this morning, didn't you?" asked Brian.

"Oh yeah, that's right, what is it called? Orvieto? I had never heard of it before. Why there?"

"I figured there will be plenty of trips to hit the main attractions. I decided to do something a little obscure. It was remarkable too, a medieval time capsule. You should go next time."

"Maybe, as long as they have a bar." Tom laughed along with the girls.

"Well, I am on a mission to find my wife an anniversary present; I'll be back in a while."

"Brian, check-in is at eight tomorrow morning, so we are good until midnight for a few drinks if you choose to imbibe. I'm coming back down to the hotel bar if you care to join me."

Now comes the tug of war, Brian thought. Ordinarily he would have said yes but today was not an ordinary day. "I don't think so, Tom, today has been a whirlwind. I think the bed is in my near future, but thanks for asking."

"Okay, suit yourself. The shuttle leaves at seven a.m. I'll meet you in the lobby then."

"Goodnight," Brian said as he made his way out the door in search of something for Maryanne. *Guys stink at this*, Brian thought. The hotel was in a business area with several shops still open. First things first–he was beyond hungry! Making it across the street to a café, and walking up to the front, there were various dishes presented under a glass counter. At least he could point and was able to pick out *abacchio alla romana*. The waiter uttered, "roast lamb." That sounded interesting. It was not long and worth the wait. Sitting inside the restaurant at a small table, Brian observed the surroundings. Mostly couples filled the dining area. Romantic accordion music was playing in the background suitable for a gondola in Venice and made him think of Maryanne. Finishing his first real dinner in Rome, it was time to find the love of his life something special, just for her.

Leaving the restaurant and strolling along the crowded sidewalk, people of all ages were walking, mingling and enjoying the cool of the evening before sleep called them home. He passed by a small courtyard where it seemed like a hundred people were gathered in small groups, many holding cones of fresh-scooped gelato. Several restaurants contributed to the aroma of evening all with outside seating covered with either umbrellas or canopies in case of rain. It seemed like every seat was taken. The sound of countless conversations echoed against the walls of the surrounding buildings. He paused to admire the sense of community. American cities seemed sterile by comparison.

Seeing all the friends and families enjoying life with joy and laughter brought on a sense of loneliness and he wished Maryanne could be with him in that moment. Pulling himself away from the scene and continuing up the street, he finally found a small jewelry store. This time he only looked at the jewelry! He had an hour before they closed and slowly scanned their selection of suitable adornments. The woman behind the counter knew a little English. "What would you recommend for a tenth anniversary?" Brian asked. He might as well have opened his wallet and said, *here, take what you want.* Brian thought, almost laughing.

She smiled and said, "What does she wear?" She wasn't much for rings or necklaces or even bracelets, but she did enjoy different earrings. That was it… a nice set of earrings with some Italian style. She steered him to a beautiful set of 18-carat-gold hoops with a half-carat of inset diamonds in each one. They were not too large; Maryanne would love them. The American Express card tacked on another twenty-five hundred dollars to the balance. He would get Hyler a doll or something at the airport. Children are much less demanding when it comes to gifts. With the goal achieved, and a full stomach, Brian started back for the hotel.

As much as Brian desired to bask in the enchantment of an evening in Rome, he was drawn to a higher enchantment of the soul. Sarah had given him God's love letter to man and it was time to start reading what it had to say. He navigated back to the room and managed to avoid any more chance encounters with people he didn't want to talk to at that moment. Quickly opening and closing the door, he fell into bed and enjoyed the first moment of relaxation since napping on the jet. The first order of business was to call Maryanne and Hyler and let them know everything was okay. With shoes off and head on the pillow, he dialed Atlanta.

It was 9:30 p.m. Rome time and 4:30 in the afternoon on the east coast of America adjusting for daylight savings time. Brian couldn't wait to hear the voices of the ones he loved. One thing was sure; he would not let on about what really happened today–that would come later. Hyler saw the number pop up on her mom's phone then Brian's face appeared identifying the caller. She grabbed the phone and answered.

"Hey Daddy! Where are you?"

"Hey Pumpkin! I am in Rome, Italy. It is beautiful. You and mom are going to come here with me one day. Would you like that?"

"That would be fun. When are you coming home?"

"I'll be home tomorrow night. I can't wait to see you!"

It was truer than she could have known. The love in his heart for her and Maryanne was at a breaking point. If he could fly out that night, he would.

"Where is your mom?"

"She is right here. I love you Daddy!" Then she would do as she always did; she gave him a hug and kiss over the phone with loud grunts and smacking lips. Brian closed his eyes and smiled.

"I love you too Kiddo, see you tomorrow."

Hyler covered the mouthpiece and said, "Dad is taking us to Italy!"

Maryanne picked up the phone. "Hey Gorgeous." Brian said before she could say anything. "I love you."

"I love you too. What's this about us going to Italy?"

"You must see this place. I'm captivated. I don't know when, but I know we will. I can't wait to see you tomorrow!"

They talked a little more. Maryanne was relieved to hear from him and especially liked the warmth in his voice.

Brian got syrupy; he couldn't help it. "Maryanne, would it be ok if I said 'I love you' about ten times in a row?"

Maryanne laughed. "What has gotten into you? Maybe you should go to Italy more often!"

"I just feel so blessed." That was not a word he would have used before. Maryanne picked it up right away.

"What do you mean by blessed?"

"I mean you and Hyler. I met an old friend today when I arrived in Rome. I might have told you about him, Jim Covino, you never met him. We used to fly together in Afghanistan. He flies for United now out of Chicago. At first it was so good to see him. I thought we were going to reminisce the glory days, as I always call them. I am not sure how it came up, but he immediately dumped on me about all his problems... divorced, with two boys and only sees them every other weekend. He was just so depressed—it depressed me! I didn't know what to say. He seemed so defeated, as if life wasn't worth living anymore. We parted ways and it took about fifteen minutes to rise out of the funk he put me in. That's what I mean by blessed. I'm blessed to have you and Hyler in my life."

"I guess I'm blessed too then." Maryanne responded.

"Let's make sure we stay blessed." Brian added.

"Okay, it's a deal," she said. "See you tomorrow. Have a safe trip, love you..."

"I love you too. Goodnight." Brian gave her a hug and kiss too, the same way Hyler did with him. Maryanne laughed as she hung up the phone.

Chapter 13:

Day Two

Brian woke up refreshed. He may have flown military and commercial jets for twenty years, but this was only the second day of his new life. There was a feeling of expectancy—even exhilaration—and he was gripped with a sense of purpose that energized his soul. Rarely remembering dreams, during the night he dreamed about the well and having a deep conversation with Sarah. She was answering all his questions—which seemed endless. It was so vivid. Brian didn't realize how prophetic the dream would be.

Before going to sleep, as Sarah suggested, he read the first three chapters from the Gospel of John. It was powerful. For the first time in his life, he read it and never questioned anything. He knew it was God's word and received it like a child. Before, even though he believed in God, his skeptical mind would have challenged everything. Not anymore. It was wonderful to read and know it as truth. It changed everything.

Those chapters made it clear: Jesus was the Word of God made flesh and everything that exists came into being through the Word. That means Jesus is not only the Son of God, but he is the creative force that brought the universe into existence. *How amazing is that? No wonder the crucifixion is such a big deal. Look who it was!* Brian thought. The same chapter says, "he came unto his own, but his own did not receive him." It was the Jews that did not receive him initially but "his own" could also mean the entire human race. Most people he knew were agnostic at best. It reminded him of what Father Gabelli had said yesterday about "the stone the builders rejected." The best part of the chapter was where it said, "to all who received him, to those who believed in his name, he gave the right to become children of God." That is what happened to him! He received Jesus. No wonder the Bible seemed so different and powerful. Jesus is the Word and now that Word was in him by the Spirit. In fact, in John chapter three, Jesus talks about being "born again" by the Spirit. Brian didn't pretend to understand how it all worked. All he knew was that there was a radical difference in his life; there must be a reason for such a transformation and this certainly explained it.

The newness of the experience was not wearing off yet as Sarah warned might happen, but the thought of interacting with everyone was unsettling. Guarding his conversion was not the issue; it was just that his faith was so new, he hoped it wouldn't be a distraction from interacting normally. Feeling like he wanted to explode, he desperately needed to talk with another believer.

Brian checked out of the room at 6 a.m. and made his way downstairs to the hotel restaurant beating the rest of the crew to fill his plate from the buffet. Eating quickly to have a few minutes with Emanuella, he finished the meal and walked toward the front lobby hoping she was there. His heart leapt seeing her behind the desk. She knew there was something special about the well. What else did she know? Was she a believer? Standing in line, she smiled and finished checking out the guest in front of him. Finally, it was his turn. "Emanuella, I am so glad to see you!"

"You must have gone to Orvieto, you look different." she said with a knowing expression.

"You don't know how different!" Brian said excitedly. "You knew there was something amazing about the well," he said with an accusing smile. "All I can say is that God was in the well. Did you know something would happen?"

"Mr. Michaels, some people have mystical encounters, but most people don't. I guess it's a matter of God's timing; it must have been your time. I am very happy for you."

"How did you learn of the well?" Brian asked.

"My cousin lives in Orvieto. I was visiting her, and we decided to check it out. I don't really know what happened but we both emerged with a strong desire to reconnect with the Church and rediscover our faith. It was unusual because both of us had become disinterested in religion a long time ago, yet we both sensed a strong spiritual pull. My cousin Maria now owns a travel agency and is involved with the city board of tourism. One of her goals is to encourage more people to visit Orvieto and maybe experience something similar."

Brian's mouth was open with shock; he couldn't believe it. "Is her last name Marinelli?"

"How did you know?"

"I met her at the shuttle. We were both on the same train. I approached her because I couldn't read any of the signs; we ended up sharing a taxi. Emanuella, that is not even half of it! You need to call her. This is unbelievable. It seems like God orchestrated everything!"

"That's incredible," she exclaimed. "I'm so happy you and Maria were able to meet."

"Emanuella, I can't thank you enough for recommending Orvieto to me. I will definitely go back, and I hope to see you again too."

"I look forward to it. Have a safe trip," she said with a big smile. Emanuella would have that smile all day just knowing she played a part in changing someone's life.

Brian now had a spiritual connection with her. It was as if they were both members of a secret society. Not that it needed to be secret, yet with most friends or acquaintances, the relationship is largely superficial. A spiritual bond is deeper and gives it purpose. He sensed the same link with Maria and Sarah. How is that possible with people he only met the previous day? Christ was the common denominator.

Brian waved goodbye to her and headed for the shuttle that would take the crew to the airport. He wished they could talk longer, but not when there was a jet that needed to leave on schedule... maybe next time.

Now the real test began...

Jenny and Suzanne were already in the van when Brian climbed in. "Hello, ladies," he said, tipping his pilot hat. "I know you're just thrilled about another ten hours in the air."

"I'd be thrilled if I had two more hours' sleep," Suzanne quipped.

"Me too," Jenny yawned.

They were young, single and a little wild, so who knows where they went or what they did last night.

Tom and Mitch got to the van at the same time, followed by six more flight attendants, fulfilling the FAA requirement of an eight-member cabin crew for their jet with a capacity of 218 passengers (two flight attendants for every 50 people). The van was full; it was time to go. Rome morning rush-hour was insane. *The safest part of the entire trip is in the air!* Brian thought.

"Where did you go last night, Tom?" asked Brian.

"Oh, nowhere special, just the hotel bar but there were lots of beautiful Italian women... who all wanted me," he laughed and winked while looking at Jenny and Suzanne.

The girls laughed and played along with his joking innuendo knowing full well they were all in their own beds by 9:00 PM. The only cure for jet lag is a good night's sleep.

"How was your friend from the Army, Mitch?" Brian asked.

"He was fine. How can you be so chipper this early in the morning? Wake me up when we get there." Mitch wasn't a morning person.

Brian wasn't either, but this morning was different.

Brian made attempts at light conversation but realized that he felt like an outsider. Before leaving Atlanta, he was just one of the guys—had a home, a wife, a daughter, a good job, and played golf on most Sundays if the weather cooperated. His language was coarse at times and retelling a crude joke was common practice. The topic of most conversations would've been the latest sports scores. You had to keep up just so there was something to talk about! Like most people going about their daily lives, he never thought much about the meaning of anything. Living life in a reasonably responsible manner, he figured to eventually retire and face whatever lies beyond this life when that day finally arrived.

But now… everything was different and had a totally new perspective on life. His thoughts, attitudes, opinions and beliefs were all turned upside down. He was connected to a higher source through his spirit, and it changed everything. It was wonderful and difficult at the same time. The process of integrating his new self with the old was going to take time. As with any journey, it was full of challenges… like the one that was about to happen.

Chapter 14:

The Unfriendly Skies

All three pilots were on the flight deck. The outer door was closed with only minutes away from pushback. They were all busy performing the necessary procedures and flight checks in preparation for take-off. Nothing was left to guesswork.

The flight schedule worked out by the three pilots was as follows: As Captain, Tom would handle take-off and fly the first break until three hours out. Mitch wanted to sleep first. After they reached "top of climb," he would find his seat in first class. Brian would sleep the second break and fly the last break. Tom would fly the second break and sleep the third, but he'd return to the flight deck and take back control for landing. Many captains like to be in charge for take-off and landings; they are the ones ultimately responsible. However, all co-pilots are required to take-off and land at least three times within a 90-day period or it is back to the simulators. Most captains will accommodate the co-pilot and yield control for that purpose. However, Tom would have the helm on this flight—neither Brian nor Mitch was under pressure to log another take-off or landing.

The flight schedule was as follows:

	Flying	Monitoring	Sleeping
1st break:	Tom	Brian	Mitch
2nd break:	Tom	Mitch	Brian
3rd break:	Brian	Mitch	Tom

The taxiway was stacked with jets from more airlines than Brian knew existed. *ITA Airways, Ryanair, EasyJet, Turkish Airlines, TAP Air Portugal,* along with all the major brands lined up 18 planes deep. Twenty minutes later, it was their turn. The flight number always changed, usually an even number on the way over and odd on the way back. Delta 54 had become Delta 55.

Brian grabbed the mic. "Delta 55—Fiumicino Tower—ready for takeoff runway two five."

Then came the reply with a thick Italian accent, "Fiumicino Tower—Delta 55—cleared for takeoff runway two five."

Tom pushed the throttle to 100% thrust and the jet lumbered down the runway rapidly gaining speed as the 400,000-pound tube (including 100,000 pounds of fuel) zoomed to 190 mph. Tom pulled up on the yoke about three thousand feet before the end of the two-mile runway. It would take another thousand feet for the wheels to leave the pavement. The jet shuddered and then smoothed out as the last wheel left the ground. At a "positive indication of climb," the wheels came up. The FAA requires a quiet cockpit until the jet reaches 10,000 feet. No discussion was allowed other than what was necessary for getting safely airborne. No one argued with the policy, the lives of all the passengers and their own were at stake.

The weather was clear. It was another beautiful day to fly as they soared to 36,000 feet. As a safety precaution, the flight back is always at a lower or higher altitude than the flight over. A mid-air collision with another Europe-bound flight was unthinkable.

Brian was already looking forward to his next trip to Rome and would check the flight schedule when he got back to Atlanta. Flying international was based on seniority. If a pilot with higher seniority bids for a particular flight, you might not get your desired destination. With lower seniority, the luck of the draw may not be in Brian's favor, and he could end up at any of the cities where the Delta had a gate waiting. But with everything else that had been going on these past two days, Brian was sure his wheels would touch down in Rome again whenever God wanted him to be there. *That was certainly a new thought!*

Once they achieved cruising altitude, Tom turned on the autopilot. They were thirty minutes into the flight.

"That's my cue boys. It's nap time." Mitch unstrapped from the jump seat and coordinated with the flight attendants to exit the flight deck. Mitch made his way to the seat in first class assigned for the pilot. Finding his ear plugs and eye mask he went right to sleep.

Unlike the trip to Rome at night, it was daytime on the return flight with plenty of light in the cockpit to read. Reading is actually forbidden by corporate policy, but some pilots do it anyway. *What can happen at thirty-six thousand feet with the autopilot on? No geese up here–just be sure to look around every few minutes,* Brian thought. Besides, Tom was at the controls and he was the captain, it would be up to him.

"Tom, I bought a few books in Orvieto, do you mind if I take a look at them?" Brian asked.

"No, that's fine. Just don't zone out on me." he laughed.

Brian was bursting at the seams to start doing more research on Orvieto and what happened to him there—but not brave enough to take out what Sarah gave him. Tom would think he had flipped his lid. He opened the flight case and found <u>The History of Orvieto</u>. *This shouldn't cause too much of a stir*, he hoped.

"What's that book about, Brian?" asked Tom.

"Well, Orvieto was such an amazing place; I decided to learn more about it. I like history and that little town was a time machine back to the Middle Ages! If you can believe it, this trip was my first time to Europe and everything about it blows me away. To have so much history in one small area is incredible. The cathedral in Orvieto was amazing. Hope to take in a few more my next time here."

"Yeah, the cathedrals are beautiful," Tom replied, "but they all look the same after a while. I have been in many of them and what strikes me is how I rarely see anyone really worshiping. Every once in a while, you might catch a Mass in progress, but only a few people attend. Sometimes an old woman comes and lights a candle in front of some shrine to Mary, but that's about it. If it wasn't for the government, none of these cathedrals would be open; the parishioners couldn't afford the upkeep. They are open because tourists from America love to come and gawk. After you've been inside one for more than a few minutes, you realize how cold, dead and empty they are. I guess that's why they have no real congregations. To tell you the truth, I think the cathedrals are dead because their religion is dead. In fact, I'll let you know exactly how I feel. I think religion is useless."

There it was. He just threw down the gauntlet. It was Brian's first challenge to his new faith. Tom made it abundantly clear how he felt about anything religious. *How should I respond to this?* Brian thought nervously. "Religion doesn't seem to be dead in America," he responded, "I see churches everywhere and some of these mega-churches have huge congregations. I don't know why the Church seems dead in Europe. Maybe it's because of too much government intrusion. Isn't it possible the Church does better when the government stays out?"

"Brian, have you been to any of these churches you talk about? Mainline denominations have been on the wane for years and losing members by the thousands. All the mega-churches have accomplished is figure out how to make church entertaining. It seems that most people go for their kids. Do they really believe the stuff they preach? They go because they think it is something they are supposed to do. They go to assuage any guilt about not teaching their kids anything themselves. How many really believe in all those Bible stories? I don't see much evidence of it myself." Tom looked away with disdain evident on his face.

Brian didn't know how to respond and hadn't been a churchgoer since high school. He wanted to challenge Tom, but was unsure of what to say. He had only read three chapters of the Bible in 20 years and that was last night, but he knew how the Word had penetrated his soul and spirit. *Here goes nothing.*

"Tom, maybe people need to actively seek God more than they do. Perhaps the entertainment church is man's idea, not God's. Isn't it possible that, even with our best intentions, we get it wrong? I don't know much about church, but I do believe in God. There must be a reason for what you just described."

Tom snapped, "Yeah, the reason is that there is no God. It's all superstition and the sooner we move on, the better the world will be. How many millions have died in the name of religion? I don't see the point in it."

Brian persevered. "I haven't been very religious over the years, but I know that is not a fair argument. How many have died in the name of atheism? Look at Joseph Stalin. He killed twenty to thirty million trying to create his god-less socialist utopia. How many more by Chairman Mao as he forced his cultural revolution on the Chinese people, another fifty million? How about Hitler? He wasn't a Christian; at best he was a mystic. World War II claimed more than fifty million lives and he deliberately exterminated twelve million, half of which were Jews. Pol Pot in Cambodia murdered two million. Atheism claimed over a hundred million lives for the twentieth century. You must go back 500 years to find the misguided murders you mentioned in the name of religion—at least for

Christianity. Islam is a different story. We are 200 years into the so-called Age of Reason, and the 20th century was the bloodiest in human history, all in the name of atheism. So, if you are going to compare atheism and religion based on the death count, then I have to admit, atheism wins by a landslide."

Brian was pleased. Knowledge of history came to his rescue. Tom took a minute to think about his next response. "Is that really a good argument for God? The fact that religion killed fewer people than atheism is not very convincing,"

"I don't know all the arguments for God, I just know that the universe is far more than just an empty void and that it didn't happen by chance. How can you look at the night sky, like we did on the way over not believe there is a God?"

"Brian, it's easy. I saw a lot of stars. I did not see God. The stars don't prove God, but they do prove the big bang theory. That's my god."

"Tom, I am an engineer by training. I study how things work, and they don't work by chance. Things work because they were designed to work, just like this jet. So, if you want to believe that all the complexity and design plainly evident within the universe and every living organism on the planet is just the result of randomness and chance, you go for it. I can't accept that."

143

"I have many reasons for not believing in God. There may be something out there, but a loving, personal God? I don't think so. My parents were both churchgoers, until my sister, Tracy, died at age ten from leukemia. Where was God then? I was 14 when it happened. My parents used to be happy people. They were never the same. It ruined my life, too. Ever since she died, they haven't been back to church, and I doubt they have uttered a single prayer. Why should they? Where was God when they needed him?

"Do you want more? Explain to me how a loving God allows such horrible things to happen to good people, I mean, people who believe in him? Why doesn't he answer their prayers for help? Where is he when the crisis comes? Oh sure, you hear the survivors of some calamity giving credit to God but what about the ones who didn't make it? Are they giving credit to God too? The ones who didn't go into work on 9/11 are praising God but how about the ones who had to jump from windows? Where was God for them?

"No, Brian, there is just way too much bad crap in the world for me to believe in a loving God. It truly is easier for me to believe we all evolved by chance, even if I can't explain how natural selection works. I admit, evolution is not a very satisfying explanation for life, but until someone gives me an answer for the questions I have raised, there is no reason for me to believe in anything else."

Brian sat and listened to Tom unload his rationale for unbelief. His hostility toward God and religion was plainly evident. Brian felt woefully unprepared to tackle his objections, and whispered a little prayer for help.

"Tom, I again must inject a disclaimer that this is not my usual line of discussion or argument on the golf course or in the cockpit. However, I have had a change of mind and heart lately. I don't know a lot about this, but maybe the answer is that if God is only a concept, only some vague abstraction, then true faith will always be out of reach." Brian was recalling some of what Sarah told him.

"Wasn't that the whole point of Jesus? It was God becoming personal, literally becoming a human being–one of us." Brian then thought about what Father Gabelli taught regarding the chalice. "What if there is something that separates us from God? And what if he cannot become real to us until it is taken out of the way? If that's true, maybe it explains why God seems so distant."

Brian was thinking about the cup and how it needed to be cleaned before God could fill it. He was dancing around the sin issue and was afraid to bring it up. It might shut down the whole conversation.

"Brian, what the hell are you talking about? What about my parents? Why did their faith not count? I don't know what you mean by personal or real. I know they believed. I thought that was all that mattered." Tom was getting agitated. He was wondering if Brian was some kind of Jesus freak. He had flown with one before and ended up arguing for hours.

Brian again ventured a response. "Can you describe the smell of a rose or the taste of a strawberry? No, you can't. A thousand words will not compare with the experience of smelling or tasting. Once you have smelled the rose or tasted the strawberry, no more words are necessary. The experience has made it real. God can be more than just a concept; he can be experienced."

Tom took the bait. "Well, how does that happen? Does he just show up like an angel out of nowhere and tap you on the shoulder? I doubt that's going to happen to me. Maybe for those who believe, but I don't."

"I am sure it is different for each person." Brian was afraid if he said too much about his experience yesterday, they would fit him for a straight jacket upon landing. "There is a verse somewhere in the Bible that says, *'Seek and ye shall find.'* Maybe that is what it's all about, that God hides himself until we start to seek him." *Or when he seeks you!* Brian thought, remembering his own encounter.

"I would sure like to know what you are talking about." Tom probed. "Bring me a rose and I'll smell it; give me a strawberry and I'll eat it. I don't know how you would experience something that can't be seen or touched."

Brian was thinking he knew just enough to make himself look like an idiot. He was not ready to talk about the well or the chalice. "Let me step back a minute and let's agree on one thing, if there is a God, it would seem logical that he can be known. The reverse is also true. If there is no God, then any belief in such must be a figment of the imagination, a myth we choose to believe in. Would you agree?"

"Sure, I can go along with that." Tom nodded.

"Here is what amazes me: I see all the animal kingdom as largely the same. They exist to serve a specific purpose within the eco system or the food chain. They don't ponder their existence or fret about their sense of worth or self-esteem. Yet man, as the evolutionist would claim, is simply one step removed from the chimpanzee. It is one enormous step! Biologists are trying all the time to prove how smart an ape may be as they attempt to narrow the evolutionary gap between man and beast. They make a big deal about training a monkey to identify colors. So what? I could put any two-year-old toddler up against any animal in a battle of wits, and I would win every time. The gap between animal and man is more like a chasm.

"What sets man apart from the animal is a sense of being, a concept of self and a free will to act outside the boundaries of simple animal instinct. Man, however, doesn't just exist; he is self-aware, he has self-consciousness, and therefore strives for meaning and purpose. And therein lies the paradox. The notion that we just evolved from other mammals doesn't make sense within an evolutionary framework. I don't see dogs or monkeys fretting over their identity. They may fight over who leads the pack but that's about it. If we came from nothing, then it would be totally illogical that the species would have ever developed a need for meaning or purpose in the first place. Randomness and chance are both devoid of either meaning or purpose, so why would man evolve with that as a need? Animals just exist; they may learn a few tricks, like a dog learning to roll over, but they do not have a sense of being.

"I contend that man's desire for personal fulfillment, accomplishment, acceptance, meaning and purpose must come from outside the ecosystem. It didn't arise from the animal kingdom. Man's ability to reason, to communicate through language, to create with his hands, to comprehend mathematics, to make music and art, to love and laugh all must come from somewhere else. These attributes are all totally unique to the human being. To suggest these enormous distinctions came about because man evolved with an opposable thumb is absurd. This is why the biblical idea that man was created in God's image makes sense. It explains the essence of purpose. Purpose requires intelligence and planning. It is derived from design. An organism cannot determine its own purpose. In my humble opinion, design and purpose must come from a higher source. This is why I believe in God and always have."

"Well, you have made some good points, but you still haven't answered all the questions I had when we began this discussion." Tom said.

"Honestly… I wasn't trying to. My premise is that, if there is a God, he should be known by his creation. And yet most people in the world believe in numerous concepts of God that range all over the board, from the energy life force of Buddhism, to the pagan pantheon of gods worshipped by the Hindus. Then there is the angry taskmaster god of Islam, who seems to love death more than life, to the God of the Jews, who required strict adherence to hundreds of different laws and annually required animal sacrifices as an atonement for sins. Then there is Christianity, built on the foundation of Judaism, in which we don't make animal sacrifices for sins, but rather Christ, God's only son, offered himself as a one-time sacrifice in our place as a divine payment for something we could never pay ourselves, and then rose again defeating death. So, the question is which one is true, and which one is false? They can't all be true!"

Brian was glad he paid attention when he took that comparative religion course in college. He remembered the basics of each one. It was all finally making sense.

"Brian, I don't get where you are going with this. I don't believe in God... period. So why should I concern myself with any of these religions?"

"I understand that, however my premise is that if there is a God, he should be known by his creation. Yet there seems to be any number of ways invented by man to somehow get to God. Yet they are all so radically different they can't all be true. However, it does not mean they are all false. Isn't it possible that, as the Bible contends, we are a fallen race and disconnected from God? In our state of disconnection, perhaps we are all like blind men groping in the darkness for something that feels like truth. What if God, understanding our situation, provided a way to find him? Shouldn't we look for it?"

"I hear what you are saying, Brian, but it doesn't give me a reason to believe. Your take on Christianity doesn't prove it's not just another invention of man." Tom was getting annoyed with the whole conversation. Most arguments about religion end up that way. He was riding with a copilot that could make a decent argument for God but couldn't answer his specific objections. The guy talked about having a personal experience but wouldn't share his own. He shook his head; it was time to change the subject.

Brian knew he couldn't take it any further without looking like a fool but felt good. He didn't back down from the fight.

"Tom, it doesn't sound like I have explained myself very well. The whole God thing is new to me. You raise some good questions, and wish I had answers. I don't know why your sister died or why bad things happen to good people, or why good things happen to bad people. Maybe God sorts all that out in the end."

"Yeah, maybe he does... I've had enough religion for one day, Brian, are you a sports fan? Did you catch the Braves game the other night?"

Their conversation soon went quiet. Brian looked out the window to the water below. Even six miles high, it was water as far as the eye could see, all the way to the horizon. It was almost as spectacular as the Milky Way Galaxy. He thought about his conversation with Tom and was happy with his line of argument given his new faith was only a day old. Then Brian realized, it wasn't just him anymore, he didn't do it alone.

A smile of knowing came to his face and whispered a prayer of thanksgiving—God had given the help requested.

Chapter 15:

Connecting the Dots

They were a third of the way home and it was time to trade places. Grabbing his two books from Orvieto, Brian switched seats with Mitch in the first-class cabin.

"Did you get any sleep?" asked Brian as they met in the doorway.

"Actually, I did and feel great, I was so tired. Hopefully my snoring didn't keep anyone up!" The truth is no one would have heard it anyway. With personal tv screens and ear buds at every seat, almost the entire cabin was zoned out. Mitch moved past Brian and took his place next to the captain.

Brian settled into the assigned seat in First Class. He wasn't tired at all. In fact, his conversation with Tom had him all wound up. He pulled out the other book purchased in Orvieto, Aquinas in the 21st Century, written by two scholars with an ecumenical approach. The book offered two points of view regarding Aquinas' contribution to theology and the core doctrines of the faith.

Brian forgot all about sleep and started to read. There were nagging questions in his mind as he flipped the pages hoping the book would offer some direction. Brian was struggling to connect the dots of his entire ordeal. He thought about all the "chance" meetings with Emanuella, Sarah, and Maria and her being able to make the connection with Father Gabelli. God was at work, but what was he missing? Why did it involve Orvieto, a well named after Saint Patrick and a chalice crafted by Saint Thomas Aquinas?

Aquinas was a fierce defender of Christian orthodoxy. Church doctrines were always being challenged. There were many heresies in his time. Most prominent was a group called the Cathars found mostly in Southern France that believed in a dualistic view of life where the material or physical world was considered evil, while the spiritual realm was good. They saw the physical body as a prison for the soul. As a result, people were encouraged to renounce the world through asceticism to free their spirits. This heretical view caused them to believe that Jesus did not enter the physical world as a man and was therefore never crucified nor resurrected but only manifested in spirit. Reincarnation was the way to ultimate salvation. However, traditional Christianity, affirmed what God said about the material world when he created it: *And God saw that it was good.* But after the fall in the garden, it needed to be redeemed which led to the cross. The Cathars traced their roots from ancient Gnosticism that emerged in the third century. Gnostics sought after hidden knowledge and focused more on esoteric and metaphysical aspects of spirituality.

They ultimately twisted or denied the central truths of Christianity.

Early Gnostic writings included the Gospel of Thomas, the Gospel of Mary Magdalene, the Gospel of Judas and other works, mostly written in the second through fourth centuries and were never considered authoritative. Matthew, Mark, Luke and John were all eyewitness accounts written in the first century. If other writings didn't match up with the eye-witness accounts, they were rejected.

Just before Aquinas was born, the Church waged a 20-year crusade (1209-1229) in the south of France, killing an estimated two hundred thousand Cathars. Some estimates are as high as a million! Many in the modern age consider it genocide. The Cathar movement was also a rebellion against oppressive and often corrupt Church rule. As they rejected the Catholic Church, they also rejected core biblical beliefs. It is not possible to defend violence and bloodshed in the name of the Church. It doesn't seem from a contemporary vantage point that the Catholic faith was under any real threat from the Cathars but then no one ever thinks that a campfire can spread into an out-of-control forest fire. That is no doubt what the Catholic authorities were trying to prevent. It doesn't justify all the violence, but it does explain the motive.

Aquinas was a champion of the Catholic doctrine of *transubstantiation* wherein the Communion wafer, known as the host, becomes the "Real Presence" of Christ, literally becoming his flesh even though the appearance doesn't change; therefore, it changes "in essence." Likewise, the wine becomes, in essence, his blood. There are many debates about this doctrine. Some Protestant views are similar in affirming the Real Presence while not going so far as transubstantiation such as Anglican, Lutheran and Methodist. They hold to a belief that the presence of Christ is *with* the elements but does not transform the elements as Catholics believe. Others hold to a more symbolic view such as Presbyterian and Baptist. Protestants also vary across the board as to how central and how often Communion should be celebrated.

Brian wasn't sure about any of this... but the idea of the Real Presence intrigued him. At the end of the day, did it really matter so long as the sacrament was received in sincerity and reverence? Brian didn't understand why the Catholic Church and perhaps other churches would not allow him to receive Communion simply because he didn't subscribe to their brand of Christianity. Shouldn't being a fellow believer in Christ be enough? He thought how Tom might use this as another objection. Would Christ be so exclusionary among those who believe?

One thing bothered Brian as he read the book. The earliest church writings such as the Didache, also known as the "Teaching of the Twelve Apostles," a document that was circulated in the late first century, does not mention anything like Transubstantiation. Communion is described as a communal meal focused on Christian fellowship. Other documents supported an early belief in the Real Presence, but not to the extent of Transubstantiation–that belief would not be codified as doctrine for another thousand years.

The term seems to have been first used by Hildebert of Tours (about 1079) and was officially adopted during the Fourth Lateran Council of 1215 convened by Pope Innocent III. In fact, it was issued as the first official pronouncement of the council to be adopted by the larger Church as sacred doctrine and was instituted precisely to combat the Cathars who were formally condemned at the same council. At the exact same time as the council, the Church was waging war against the Cathars who denied all aspects of the eucharist.

Brian thought of the law of unintended consequences. Maybe the Pope thought it was a good idea at the time to combat false doctrine, but now the Communion meal, the very sacrament established by Jesus to foster unity and fellowship among fellow believers, as practiced in the First Century, had become a point of division simply because people can't agree on what it means. *How ridiculous is that?* Brian thought. Leave it to man to complicate something that was meant to be so simple.

Aquinas was a great thinker, but something was missing. His was a time when laborious arguments were made using the philosophic tradition of the Greek masters. Medieval philosophy is essentially theological. Godless existential philosophy wasn't even considered. They didn't debate things that were not inherently Christian. Aquinas and others used the logical techniques of ancient philosophers to address theological questions and points of doctrine. It explained why Aquinas admired Aristotle so much. He loved his style of argument with the use of logic, analysis and dialectic (dialogue and discussion) to discover truth.

It was important but lacking. What was lacking? The fullness of the Spirit! All this theology and philosophy is like a dry sponge. Brian peered out the window trying to figure it all out. That is when he sensed it. It was not a voice in his spirit, but more like a thought that was planted in his mind. He recalled a verse of Scripture he learned in youth group over twenty years ago. *Whosoever shall call upon the name of the Lord shall be saved* (Rom 10:13). Amazed that it came to mind after all these years, the meaning was obvious. Christ excludes no one who comes to him in faith.

What is the connection to the well? He remembered Sarah's words where Jesus said, *out of your innermost being shall flow rivers of living water* (John 7:38). Adding to what he just realized, the message became clear; the fullness of

God's Spirit is available to anyone who calls upon the name of Christ. *That was it!* Brian thought. The doctrine of the Real Presence is also a metaphor! It represents the transformation that occurs when Christ changes the heart of a believer. That's what happened to him. He was transformed by the Real Presence of Christ, not in a wafer, but as a spiritual reality. This had to be it. The fact that he's not Catholic indicates God wants all to know: *Everyone is invited to drink from the well of salvation and experience the fullness of His Spirit.*

This in no way minimizes the importance of Communion. But he couldn't imagine the sacrament was ever intended to be a barrier to faith. Jesus didn't begin his ministry until the dove descended upon him as a visible sign of the Spirit. The Apostles had to wait until the Day of Pentecost before they could transform the world. Everything points to the transforming power of the Spirit.

Anyone who comes to Christ in faith can drink to the full. No one is turned away. Certain branches of organized religion may in ignorance turn away those who don't buy into their brand, but Jesus excludes no one. Brian didn't find the answer in an ornate cathedral, nor in the Papal Palace but at the bottom of a 200-foot well. It is the gift of living water available to all for the asking.

Chapter 16:

The Aquinas Revelation

Brian was thrilled with all this new understanding of what happened in Saint Patrick's Well. However, it didn't explain the chalice and the connection to Saint Thomas. Brian continued to read about Aquinas. There must be an answer.

Thomas was a prolific writer and authored over forty books in his lifetime, comprising over eight million words. His final work was called *Summa Theologica*. The work is an entire theology of Christ comprising over three thousand articles. They were set up to answer hundreds of questions posed to challenge the faith. He never finished the treatise and stopped writing in Part Three at the nineteenth question. It was a question dealing with penance. Why did he stop?

It is said he had a vision from God that was so powerful and so transforming, he never wrote again. Following a Mass on December 6, 1273, the Feast Day of St. Nicholas, he said, "All that I have written seems to me like straw compared to what has now been revealed to me." Three months later he died.

Brian wondered, what was revealed to him and why did he stop writing at penance? There is no official answer to this question. Brian knew the answer. Straw is dry and brittle. What Thomas knew was lacking in all his writing was the power of the Spirit, often symbolized by water. No amount of theology or religion can substitute for being filled with the Spirit manifested as love. Without the Spirit and without love, everything is dry and brittle, just like straw.

Why did he stop at penance? The answer would come 241 years later through the revelation of another man of God, Martin Luther. Luther's principal complaint was the Church's preoccupation with "works" as a means of salvation. This was perversely manifested through the selling of indulgences and requiring penance for sin. Luther's revelation was that faith in Christ alone was sufficient for salvation, not works, not the payment of indulgences and not penance. To suggest penance was necessary for salvation is to say that Christ's death on the cross was not enough, that it was insufficient. Yet Jesus said right before he died, "It is finished." Regarding this same question, his followers specifically asked Jesus *What must we do to do the works God requires? Jesus answered, The work of God is this: to believe in the one he has sent* (John 6:28-29). Jesus makes no mention of "works" as a requirement for salvation.

Luther claimed that the Catholic Church had imposed a "tyranny" on the people by turning everything, even the sacraments, into works, and by "doing" them people were saved rather than by faith alone as he had come to believe. Luther had been transformed by the power of the Word. He singlehandedly translated the Scriptures into the German language. In the process he discovered the verse that changed his life.

For by grace are ye saved through faith; and that not of yourselves: it is the gift of God: Not of works, lest any man should boast (Eph 2:8-9).

The very next verse puts things in the proper order: *For we are his workmanship, created in Christ Jesus unto good works, which God hath before ordained that we should walk in them* (Eph 2:10).

Isn't it obvious? Brian thought. Clearly, it is not works that saves us, but faith. Yet we are called to do good works as the Spirit of God leads and empowers us. *Why do so many get the cart before the horse? Why is this so hard to figure out?* Brian wondered.

Despite Aquinas' inclination towards complicated theology, the Chalice of Truth was the opposite. It encapsulated the Gospel message and was free of Church dogma. The power of the chalice is derived from its simplicity and truth.

Through his writings, Thomas created a theological framework, perhaps necessary at the time, to combat religious

161

heresy, but it focused on works and lacked the power of faith. Luther restored faith as the primary ingredient needed for salvation, but he lacked an understanding of the Spirit.

The end-time message of the Chalice of Truth merged in Brian's mind with his own experience in the well. He came to understand something profound and imminent. God would soon be pouring out his Spirit on the world in greater measure as the end of the age draws near.

Without the Word, there can be no abiding faith as Luther discovered. Without the Spirit, manifested as love, religion becomes like straw as Aquinas discovered. They all go together, and they will all be necessary as believers enter a period of global transition and even tribulation.

Brian sat looking out the window of the jet to the water below. He was immersed in his thoughts and transformed by the power of this revelation. Why was it given to him? He would know soon enough.

Chapter 17:

Coming Home

Brian fumbled for his car keys, opened the rear door, put his flight case on the seat and climbed behind the wheel of a silver Lexus LS, the one thing he loved almost as much as flying an F-16. With 380 horsepower, it could rocket to 60 mph in less than six seconds. Pilots love speed. Pressing the button for the keyless ignition, the motor came to life with a familiar roar. He took a deep breath; it was good to be back in Atlanta. He sat for a minute and found the speed dial on his iPhone that would find Maryanne, wherever she was.

"Hey baby, I'm home. Did you miss me?"

"I always miss you. How was your flight?"

"Nothing unusual." *Is not telling the truth the same as a lie?* He wasn't going to discuss anything of substance over the phone.

"I got something for you in Rome," he teased.

"Yeah? Will I like it?"

"I sure hope, so or my American Express card will be very sad!"

"Did you spend a ton of money?" Maryanne asked a little concerned.

"You'll find out when the bill comes. How's Hyler?" Brian changed the subject.

"She's in the other room doing homework."

Brian couldn't wait to see his little family. "I'll see you in about thirty minutes... love you."

"I love you too," Maryanne responded with a curious tone. There was something different in his voice and she didn't know what to make of it. He sounded warmer, more genuine, like last night on the phone. Maryanne shrugged it off. She would find out soon enough.

"Hyler, your dad will be home soon. Go get that picture you drew so you can give it to him when he comes in the door." Hyler had an artistic flair. She also had a connection that neither parent realized.

Brian mused as he cruised along the interstate I85 toward Peachtree City, a conclave for the airline industry servicing Atlanta's sprawling airport. Hartsfield-Jackson International boasts the most flights daily of any airport in the world. Looking up in the sky he could see a dozen jets in the pattern waiting to land. Brian was proud to be part of a modern-day miracle.

He thought about Maryanne and how he might explain the events of his first international flight, about Orvieto and Saint Patrick's Well, about Sarah, Maria and Emanuella, about Father Gabelli and Saint Thomas's Chalice and how it came into his possession and what he must do with it. It was overwhelming and required a distraction.

Brian turned on the radio—there were two Christian stations on the FM dial that he never listened to… until now and felt blessed to live in area with enough Christians to support two stations! He didn't know a single song; they were all new to him but loved the lyrics. Music for the soul and spirit was just what was needed.

Brian pulled into the three-car garage and parked in between Maryanne's white Chevy Tahoe and the golf cart. Nearly everyone owned a golf cart in this town. Peachtree City has over 90 miles of bike and cart paths linking all the shopping areas and subdivisions. Most paths go through the woods, officially known as green belt areas attracting bikers and joggers but the dominant vehicle had a Club Car logo. Hyler would be expecting a ride later. She would sit on his lap and steer as they hit a top speed of 20 mph.

Grabbing his flight case and roller bag, Brian struggled through the side door leading to the kitchen. "Hi Honey," Maryanne purred as she hugged him tight with a small kiss. Brian dropped his bags. "Hi, Daddy!" Shouted Hyler as she ran and jumped into his arms. She was almost nine, but she still liked to be picked up and twirled around. She kissed him on the cheek while he sat her down on the counter. "I have something for you, Daddy." She slipped back off the counter and brought the picture over from the table. Brian was still standing in the kitchen. "I drew you a fountain."

Brian held it up to see it better. It showed water flowing up through the top and collecting in a pool below surrounded by a courtyard. Brian was taken aback. It was reminiscent of the one at Three Fountains Abbey in Rome. "Why did you draw this? It's beautiful. Did you see it in a book?"

"No, I just saw it in my mind. I had a dream about it the night before too."

"It's very pretty, Hyler. Thank you. I love you sooooo much!"

Hyler was excited, but Mom was puzzled. *Why was Brian so taken with this picture versus any other picture she had drawn over the years?*

"I'll be right back down; I need to get out of this uniform." Brian put his flight case in the den and took the roller bag with him to the bedroom. Blue jeans and a T-shirt sounded great. He thought about Hyler's fountain; how could that just come into her mind? It must be related to everything that had gone on over the past few days.

Brian realized that everything that had happened over the past forty-eight hours was confirmed through his 8-year-old daughter. *A dry well or an empty fountain is useless.* Hyler's picture was an affirmation of what he had experienced. Brian looked up at the ceiling and said a simple prayer: "Thank you, Lord. Help me to take the next step. Help me to explain all this to Maryanne and may you help her to receive it. Amen."

Brian bound down the stairs with renewed energy and excitement. The sense of exhilaration in his spirit from knowing that the Creator of the universe just conveyed a message through his daughter was mind-boggling. He didn't know what was coming next but knew it would be an adventure and was willing to go wherever it might lead.

"Hey, Gorgeous, what are you cooking up for us?"

"You sure are chipper. You're not your usual grumpy self after a trip, especially a long one. You must have really enjoyed Rome."

Maryanne was a terrific cook, and he always admired the way she could move around the kitchen with several things going on at once. The chicken was baking, the rice was simmering, the vegetables were steaming, all planned and timed so it would come together perfectly. Everything was under control, as usual. This was her flight deck, and she was the pilot. Brian didn't dare get in her way, or something might crash.

"How much time before dinner?"

"About ten minutes."

"I have something for you. I should really do this over a fancy dinner, but I can't wait. I want to give this to you now." He removed from his pocket a small, gift-wrapped box, and presented it to Maryanne as if it contained the crown jewels. She smiled. It had been a while since Brian surprised her with a gift.

"What did you get me?" she asked as she handled the package. She always liked to savor surprises. On Christmas day, she would open her presents last to appreciate the moment. Teasing Brian, she shook the package to hear what was inside and then sniffed it.

"Open it before the food burns." Brian laughed.

Opening the box, she found a most beautiful set of diamond-inlaid earrings. Catching her breath, she was stunned. "Oh, Brian, these are beautiful!"

She turned and gave him a hug and a big kiss on the lips.

"Ewwww!" Hyler cringed.

"Happy tenth anniversary, Honey. I know it's a week early, but I couldn't wait." Brian smiled as he and Hyler set the table, Maryanne finished the cooking, and they all took their places for the meal.

Brian had a sense of guilt come over him. For the first time since high school, he thought of blessing the food and wanted to give thanks, not just for the food, but for everything. He bit his tongue; it was too soon to drop this on Maryanne.

Dinner was terrific, as usual. Afterward, Brian offered to help with the dishes. "What's gotten into you? You're acting very strange," she said with a smile. "Is this what Europe does to people? They're not grumpy, they bring presents, they help with the dishes... well, I'll take it!"

Hyler had climbed onto the counter and was looking sad with an exaggerated frown. Brian looked at her and got the message. "Oh, so you want something too?"

Hyler cheered right up. "Did you bring me a present?"

Brian went into the den, opened his flight case and pulled out a porcelain, costumed doll of Italy wearing an apron with a village scene embroidered on the front. It represented "the old country" and captured some of the traditional culture. Brian returned to the kitchen with the doll behind his back.

"Close your eyes. I brought you something that can only be found in Italy."

Opening her eyes. "It's beautiful, Daddy!" She hugged the doll, which would one day become a treasure. Maryanne sighed and was happy too. She loved these family moments, especially this one! The earrings were perfect, and Brian was different, but in a good way.

"Okay, let's go for a golf cart ride before it gets too dark!" Brian said. The cart had a windshield, lights, and even a canopy in case of rain. The destination was a secret until they figured it out. Hyler sat in Brian's lap to steer and waved as other carts out for an evening ride passed by. It didn't take long for Hyler to realize where they were headed.

"Are you taking us out for ice cream?" she asked excitedly.

"Yep, I sure am. You're special, so you get a special treat."

Hyler was smiling from ear to ear. She loved her dad so much but hated it when he traveled. The empty chair at the table always made her feel lonely but she was happy now that her dad was back and was about to get happier as she picked out her favorite flavor—Swiss Chocolate mixed with a Reese's Peanut Butter Cup.

After enjoying their cavity-causing treats, they strolled along by the storefronts in a downtown area known as the Avenue. It was mid-May and the weather was warm. Maryanne took Hyler to Gap Kids. "I'll meet you two at the bookstore," Brian said and walked on to discover the next clue.

Brian didn't know what to look for, but felt drawn to the religious section, an area he had always avoided. There were so many books and Bibles and so many translations. He would just stick with Sarah's Bible for the time being, but needed other sources for research. Scanning the shelves, he found a Bible dictionary and a Strong's Concordance that would allow him to do detailed word searches. Sure, it could all be found online, but Brian was old school, and wanted something he could hold, feel and smell not to mention being able to underline, bracket, or make a note in the margin. He was excited and felt like a student again. As he was standing at the checkout counter, his little family walked through the door.

Maryanne looked at his purchase. "Those are some huge books!"

"I need to read up on some things that grabbed my interest in Rome. I'll tell you more about it later," he said.

"Well, Rome certainly had a big impact on you!"

"Just wait 'til I tell you about everything that happened." Brian quipped.

Maryanne wondered what that meant but decided to wait before jumping into a deep conversation... *those books looked serious!*

Chapter 18:

The Discussion

Hyler was getting ready for bed. For the first time in a long time, Brian wanted to read to her. She was excited. *Daddy hardly ever does this*, she thought. It's hard to form habits and patterns when you are gone all the time. Routines that are always interrupted don't remain routine for very long.

Brian picked out a collection of Bible stories for children. It was a single volume book filled with colorful drawings. No doubt almost every home with kids had a book like this somewhere. Someone probably gave it to the new parents as a gift when Hyler was born. As far as Brian knew, it had been opened once or twice at most.

"What story would you like to read tonight?"

"I haven't seen this book in a long time, Daddy." She flipped through the pages going from Old Testament stories to New and stopped at a picture of a woman holding a bucket, standing next to a well. Jesus was sitting beside her. "What is this story?"

This can't be happening, Brian thought. She had picked out a story known as the 'Woman at the Well'. It was the same story Sarah mentioned halfway down Saint Patrick's

Well in Orvieto. It was natural for a little girl to pick out a picture-story with a woman in it. Maybe it was because she painted a picture of a fountain. But still, what were the odds?

Brian began reading to her. Maryanne came to the door of Hyler's room mid-story. "Brian, are you ok? We've all had a great time since you got home, but you're so different. What's gotten into you?"

"Honey, I'll tell you all about it after this story. I'll be done in a few minutes." She got the clue that Brian wanted time alone with Hyler.

The Bible text read as follows from John 4:7-14 (NKJV):

A woman of Samaria came to draw water. Jesus said to her, "Give Me a drink." For His disciples had gone away into the city to buy food. Then the woman of Samaria said to Him, "How is it that You, being a Jew, ask a drink from me, a Samaritan woman?" For Jews have no dealings with Samaritans.

*Jesus answered and said to her, "If you knew the gift of God, and who it is who says to you, 'Give Me a drink,' you would have asked Him, and He would have given you **living water.**"*

174

The woman said to Him, "Sir, You have nothing to draw with, and the well is deep. Where then do You get that living water? Are You greater than our father Jacob, who gave us the well, and drank from it himself, as well as his sons and his livestock?"

*Jesus answered and said to her, "Whoever drinks of this water will thirst again, but whoever drinks of the water that I shall give him will never thirst. But the water that I shall give him will become in him a **fountain of water** springing up into everlasting life."*

"Daddy, did you hear that? Jesus said that his water is living water, and it would spring out of us like a fountain! That must be why I drew the fountain. I dreamed about it. God must want us to have that living water. How do we get it?"

Brian was in a daze. One Bible story and Hyler was ready to drink living water. God had already prepared her in a dream. *Okay, here it goes.*

"Hyler, do you know that God loves you very much?"

"Yes, I think he does, except when I'm bad."

"No, God loves you all the time, good or bad. I love you all the time too. I may get upset with you, but I never stop loving you. God is the same way. I can't explain to you why it was necessary, perhaps when you are older, but if someone gave his life for you, would that prove that he loved you?"

"Yes, it sure would."

"Well, that is what Jesus did for you and for me and for the whole world. He died on a cross and then rose from the dead three days later and overcame death for us. Because he lives, we can live with him forever too. Like an enemy, death has been defeated. When you die, you don't just go into the ground; you will go to be with Jesus and live in his Kingdom forever, some call it heaven. All Jesus asks us to do is believe in him and ask him into our lives by faith. Then he promises to give us the living water we read about."

"I want that."

Brian led Hyler in a prayer to ask Jesus into her life and to be filled with his Spirit. When they were done, she had a smile from ear to ear. "Can we do this every night?"

Brian laughed. "Sweetheart, you don't need to do this every night. Once Jesus is in your life, he is there for good unless you kick him out. No one can ever take this away from you! He loves you very much, even more than your mom or I could love you. You see, Mom gave birth to you, and we are raising you as our daughter, but God is the one who created you. Before you go to sleep, thank Jesus for coming into your life and ask him to give you sweet dreams. Good night,

Honey. I love you." Hyler gave her dad a hug and a kiss. Brian got up to leave and stood outside her door. He heard Hyler say in a soft whisper, "Thank you Jesus for my mom and dad, and thank you for coming into my life. Please let me have sweet dreams. Good night."

Brian smiled and prepared himself for the most challenging conversation of his life. He prayed while walking slowly down the hall. "Lord, help me explain all this to Maryanne and help her to receive it the way Hyler just did! Thank you for preparing Hyler's heart. I know you are in all of this, Lord. Thank you so much." He crept into the master bedroom and braced himself.

"Well, it's about time!" Maryanne exclaimed, half joking and half serious. "I want to hear what this new attitude is all about. You mentioned something at the bookstore tonight. What happened in Rome that brought you home a different person?"

Maryanne was lying on her side of the bed, propped up on pillows with the TV on mute. Brian sat down on his side of the bed and faced her. "When I arrived in Rome, I had all day to kill as part of my layover and decided to do something non-touristy. The woman at the desk recommended a small town about an hour away by train called Orvieto. So, I went, and it was wonderful—like being transported back through time to the Middle Ages. What happened to me involved three

177

women, a deep well built by Pope Vincent the Seventh in the 1500s, and the Catholic Church's most famous theologian, Saint Thomas Aquinas. Do I have your interest yet, other than being miffed about the three women?"

"Yes…" she said cautiously. "I want to hear about the three women first."

"Let's start with Emanuella. She was working the hotel desk and recommended I visit Orvieto and was the first to say I should check out Saint Patrick's Well. The second is Maria. I met her at the bus station where a shuttle came to take passengers from the train into Orvieto. I needed someone who could translate the signs, and it turned out she spoke excellent English. I learned she runs a travel agency and promotes tourism for the city of Orvieto." Brian didn't mention that they had shared a cab. That might not go over so well. "She also told me about the well built in the 1500s by order of the Pope. I can't tell you every detail, but I can tell you this much–God was in that well." Maryanne gave him a quizzical look.

"What are you talking about? God is everywhere. He doesn't live in a well," she said.

Brian knew this was going to be difficult, if not impossible to explain. "Um, I know, but maybe he shows up in certain places for a reason. Let me go on. This well is 42 feet wide and 200 feet deep with two stairways, one up and one down, and it looks exactly like a double helix, you know, the DNA molecule. It is truly a marvel. As soon as I took my first step into the well, 'it' started. I was bombarded with thoughts of God. Somehow and someway, I had a strong sense of his presence. The feeling or whatever it was grew stronger the further I went down into the well. It was powerful... but I wasn't scared or anything. It's hard to explain.

"There was a woman in front of me; Sarah Foxworth. She is the third woman in the story and is an American from Dallas. She lives in Italy but works with Texas Instruments. I asked her if she was feeling what I was feeling. As it turned out, Sarah is a strong Christian, a student of Scripture, and even went to seminary for a while. She explained so clearly what was going on in my soul and ended up giving me a Bible that just happened to be in her briefcase. Is it just coincidence that Sarah was right there when I needed someone to explain what was going on?

"Maryanne, I don't know what you think about all this. I know we haven't talked much about church or God, but in the middle of Saint Patrick's Well I asked Jesus to come into my life. All I can tell you is that He did. When you asked me earlier, what's gotten into me... now you know. I'm truly different and it's amazing. I have been on cloud nine ever since yesterday morning when it happened."

179

Maryanne ignored the whole Jesus-thing, but sensed there was more to the story, "Is there anything else?"

Brian looked sheepish. "Yeah, quite a bit, actually. This all happened about halfway down the well. Sarah had to leave for a meeting. I felt the urge to go all the way down to the bottom. That's when it really happened. There were paper cups so people could drink the water. I had the cup in my hand when suddenly I heard a voice in my spirit say, *Drink deep.* I filled the cup and savored it like wine and when I was done, I heard the voice again say, *The water is my Word.* As soon as I finished the cup—I can't explain how or why—but I was filled with an overpowering sense of joy and praise. It was incredible. I encountered God in a way that was real and wonderful."

Maryanne didn't know how to take all this. She wanted to believe him but part of her was cynical too. Was this just another interest or hobby that would fade like all the others? She held her tongue and simply asked, "And then what?"

The hard part was coming up–explaining the chalice. "I stumbled into a jewelry store looking to buy something for our tenth anniversary but was immediately drawn to something else. Pacella's had all kinds of beautiful hand-crafted plates, glasses, and pottery, but in a special display case was a shimmering gold chalice. I was holding the paper cup in my hand from the well and wanted something special to put it in. The chalice would be perfect. It turns out it was a replica of one commissioned by Saint Thomas Aquinas, the great theologian of the Catholic Church during the 1200s. I had to have it."

"How much was it?" Maryanne asked with a guarded tone.

"Do I have to tell you?" Brian was trying to act cute to soften the blow.

Maryanne just nodded her head.

"It was ten thousand dollars."

Maryanne gasped and sat straight up. "What?! You make one trip to Europe, and you come back with a ten-thousand-dollar mug?" She was shocked.

Brian had already prepared for the discussion and had moved the flight case from the den to the bedroom. Opening it up, he pulled out the canvas bag given to him by Father Gabelli and slowly unwrapped the chalice, revealing the gold cup which shimmered in the soft light of the bedroom. Maryanne gasped again. It was magnificent.

Brian pulled out the paper cup from inside the chalice. "I don't know if I will ever have a similar experience, but I wanted something worthy of what happened."

"If it's any consolation, it's worth far more than what I paid. In fact, with the price of gold these days, its face value alone is easily worth what I paid, but its true value is far more."

"How do you know?" she asked in a doubtful tone. Maryanne was still in shock over the cost.

"Remember Maria, the travel agent I met at the train station? I went to her office after I bought the chalice, and she helped me locate an old Jesuit priest in Rome. He knew about the chalice and could help explain everything. I immediately set out to find him at Three Fountains Abbey. You see all these inscriptions? They are etched in Aramaic, not Latin. He helped translate all of them for me. According to him, what was thought to be a replica may be an original version commissioned by Aquinas himself. No one can know for sure, but it is much older than any of the other replicas. The original chalice has been lost for centuries; the replicas were made from drawings kept in the Papal Palace in Orvieto. Since the original is thought to be lost, it's possible that this one may even be the original! It could be worth ten times what I paid." He didn't try to explain the difference between the Aramaic and Latin versions. It would just make it more complicated. Neither did he tell her that he had spent half the day with Maria. That would come later.

Maryanne was getting more comfortable with it. Maybe it wasn't a total waste of money.

"Is that it?" She asked, hoping there weren't any more bombshells to explode.

"Well, there is the story of what all these inscriptions mean, but I think that will keep for another day. Honey, I am a changed man." Brian said as he earnestly searched her face. "I have never been more excited about anything. It feels like Christmas Day for me."

Maryanne didn't know what to say. She returned her husband's gaze and took a deep breath. "Maybe we can try church, especially for Hyler. I know we've talked about it before."

"About Hyler," Brian injected. "I had a wonderful time reading a Bible story to her. What totally astonished me is how the fountain she drew looked so much like the one in the courtyard of Three Fountains Abbey. That can't just be a coincidence! And, get this, the story she picked out, and I promise I did not help her, is called the Woman at the Well. Can you believe it? She asked Jesus into her life tonight and she was very excited."

"You don't waste any time. Are you going to convert me now, too?" Maryanne asked with obvious sarcasm.

"No, but maybe we can visit a church and see how it goes?"

That was okay–Maryanne could handle that. All this talk about Jesus so suddenly was making her nervous. However, she was intrigued by the positive changes Brian exhibited. Maybe there was something real to this after all. Even Hyler seemed to be tuned in. She was wary but interested. Brian may have wasted his money on some strange chalice, but the earrings were beautiful.

"Can we talk about all this tomorrow?" She touched the jewels now gracing her earlobes. "Aren't we supposed to be celebrating our anniversary?" she asked with a flirty look.

Brian breathed a huge sigh of relief; she didn't kill him!

Chapter 19:

Digging Deep

Brian had three days off before the next trip. He checked with Crew Scheduling and discovered Barcelona was next. He was mildly disappointed, yet hopeful of getting back to Rome in the next month or so but Barcelona sounded nice too. In fact, anywhere in Europe would be a new experience... but his heart longed for Rome.

He greeted Hyler in the morning as she came down the stairs. "Hey Pumpkin, did you sleep okay?"

"Yes, and I said that prayer like you told me to. Can we read another story tonight?"

"Absolutely, girl! You and I are going to learn a lot about the Bible together. Is that okay?"

"That sounds fun, Daddy. I have friends that go to church. Are we going to go now?"

She looked at her mom, who was making herself a bowl of cereal. "Don't look at me; that's your father's decision."

"Well, I guess the answer is yes... under one condition."

"What's that?" asked Hyler.

"Your mother has to promise to go even if I am on a trip. My schedule won't always let me be here, but if we're going to join a church, we need to be committed and involved." Brian was looking at Maryanne as he spoke.

"Okay, fine. I just hope we can find a good church with a good program for Hyler."

"We will; I have no doubt."

Maryanne took Hyler to school and would be gone the rest of the morning to the gym and onto the grocery store. Maryanne didn't work. It was a luxury of being a pilot's wife, but she volunteered at the school several days a week. Maryanne taught for a year after they were married, but when Hyler was born, she never went back. Brian didn't care as long as they could afford it. Flying international helped, but with the cost of everything going up, it was becoming a harder choice, and it was something they would have to pray about. *Now that was a new thought!*

Brian felt a sense of anticipation. This was his first real quiet time since the hotel room in Rome. After a long trip, it was such a pleasure to be back in his familiar den, known as the "wood room" with light oak paneling and comfortably worn leather furniture. Living out of a suitcase makes one appreciate home. Like a refuge, he felt embraced by the love of his wife and the wonder of an eight-year-old daughter who loved him "sooooo much." He breathed in the peace and was so relieved that Maryanne didn't flip out and even seemed interested in the story.

Brian opened his flight case and placed the Chalice of Truth on the fireplace mantle and began to study it. He found Father Gabelli's notes and repeated the words, "Chalice of Truth," and contemplated again the deep spiritual principles revealed by this simple vessel–how the marble represented the stone the builders rejected and how so many people reject Christ. Brian realized that he, too, had been a rejecter until his experience in the well. He claimed to be a Christian for so many years, but it was only a façade, nothing like his newfound faith and marveled at his own transformation.

God's Spirit was again speaking to his spirit. Brian began saying, "Thank you Jesus, thank you Lord" repeatedly, just like in the well. Walking from the mantle to the sofa, he sat down and leaned over with hands drawn up to his face and began to weep tears of thankfulness, tears of joy, and tears of praise as he thought about how these truths had become spiritual realities in his own soul.

Then he heard it–the same voice in his spirit he had heard in Orvieto. *You will be my Cup Bearer.* Sitting motionless and knowing what he heard, he started to repeat it to himself, "You will be my Cup Bearer." What did that mean? What is a Cup Bearer? Brian stood up, straightened his clothes, and turned on his laptop. It was as if he received marching orders. He didn't know what it meant but was determined to find out.

Apparently, there were several cup bearers in the Bible. *They were men who served the king.* That was a powerful thought! Solomon had cup bearers in his court. Joseph, the son of Jacob, rose from slavery in Egypt to become the cup bearer to Pharaoh. Nehemiah was the cup bearer to the king of Persia. In all cases, they were positions of authority, respect and prominence. The function was to pour the wine for the king and his guests. The cup bearer would taste it first to make sure it was suitable.

That was good for starters, but how did it relate to what he was called to do? Brian got out his new Strong's Concordance and started by finding all the references for how the word "cup" is used in the Bible.

Sitting at the desk with Sarah's Bible, he began looking up verse after verse. His spirit moved within him as he read the Word, just like the night in Rome when he read the first three chapters of John. Once it started, he couldn't stop. With each verse, there was a need to read the surrounding verses to understand the context. He felt like a spiritual detective tracking down clues to solve a great mystery; it was fascinating. A week ago, nothing could have been more boring.

The most famous verse using the word "cup" is in the 23rd Psalm. Even Brian knew that one.

*You prepare a table before me in the presence of my enemies. You anoint my head with oil; my **cup** overflows.*

A verse the Jews recite during the Passover meal is from Psalm 116:13

*I will take the **cup** of salvation and will call upon the name of the Lord.*

Brian remembered what Sarah said about *the well of salvation.* With this verse, the metaphor changed to the *cup of salvation;* was that the meaning of the chalice?

Brian continued to find more references and found the ones Father Gabelli had mentioned regarding the cup of God's wrath and the judgment of wayward Israel as they followed false idols or judgement upon enemy nations that persecuted them.

*You will be filled with drunkenness and sorrow, the **cup** of ruin and desolation* (Ezekiel 23:33).

*This is what the LORD, the God of Israel, said to me: "Take from my hand this **cup** filled with the wine of my wrath*

189

and make all the nations to whom I send you drink it" (Jeremiah 25:15-18).

*Awake, awake! Rise up, O Jerusalem, you who have drunk from the hand of the LORD the **cup** of his wrath* (Isaiah 51:17).

Brian sensed there was something else he was supposed to find. Moving to the New Testament where Jesus was railing against the pretense of the Pharisees.

*Woe to you, teachers of the law and Pharisees, you hypocrites! You clean the outside of the **cup** and dish, but inside they are full of greed and self-indulgence. Blind Pharisee! First clean the inside of the **cup** and dish, and then the outside also will be clean* (Matthew 23:25-26).

That's exactly what Father Gabelli taught; the **cup** is a metaphor for our souls. It was the teachers of the law and the Pharisees, the most "religious" people of their day, who rejected Christ and called for his crucifixion. In their pride, they thought they were already good enough, but Jesus peered into their souls and saw all the filthiness of human sin. What really angered Jesus was the hypocrisy of claiming to be so holy while on the inside they were just as sinful as anyone else. They thought their religious status somehow made them more worthy before God. The very next verse indicates what Jesus thought of their religious hypocrisy.

Woe to you, teachers of the law and Pharisees, you hypocrites! You are like whitewashed tombs, which look beautiful on the outside but on the inside are full of dead men's bones and everything unclean. In the same way, on the outside you appear to people as righteous but on the inside you are full of hypocrisy and wickedness (Matthew 23:27-28).

People need to clean the inside of their cups, which is something that can only be accomplished through Christ. Brian realized this not only applied to the Pharisees of Jesus' day, but to everyone who thinks they have no need for Christ— that somehow, they are "good enough" on their own merits. The people in this story were religious Jews who spent their lives abiding by the law. If they weren't good enough, who was? That was Jesus' point; *all have sinned and fall short of the glory of God* (Rom 3:23). They couldn't accept Jesus because they couldn't accept their own sinfulness. They thought they were clean through their pretense of religion. Self-righteous pride became their downfall and blinded them from seeing their own promised Messiah right in front of their eyes!

Next Brian read where Jesus instituted the Last Supper with the Apostles on the night he was betrayed. It reads:

*Then he took the **cup**, gave thanks and offered it to them, saying, "Drink from it, all of you. This is my blood of* *the covenant, which is poured out for many for the forgiveness of sins* (Matthew 26:27-29).

The chalice he now possessed was certainly an implement for serving the communion wine, but that was too obvious, it had to be something else. Nothing seemed to resonate as the answer until it did...

Then Jesus came with them to a place called Gethsemane, and said to the disciples, "Sit here while I go and pray over there." And He took with Him Peter and the two sons of Zebedee (James and John), and He began to be sorrowful and deeply distressed. Then He said to them, "My soul is exceedingly sorrowful, even to death. Stay here and watch with me.

He went a little farther and fell on His face, and prayed, saying, **O My Father, if it is possible, let this CUP pass from me; nevertheless, not as I will, but as you will.**

Then He came to the disciples and found them sleeping, and said to Peter, "What! Could you not watch with me one hour? Watch and pray, lest you enter into temptation. The spirit indeed is willing, but the flesh is weak."

Again, a second time, He went away and prayed, saying, **"O My Father, if this CUP cannot pass away from me unless I drink it, your will be done."** *And He came and found them asleep again, for their eyes were heavy.*

So He left them, went away again, and **prayed the third time, saying the same words.** *Then He came to His disciples and said to them, "Are you still sleeping and resting? Behold, the hour is at hand, and the Son of Man is being betrayed into the hands of sinners. Rise, let us be going. See, my betrayer is at hand."* (Matt 26:36-46)

Brian prayed for wisdom to understand. In this scene, Jesus was in the Garden of Gethsemane following the Passover meal and his last supper with the disciples. He knew what would happen tomorrow. Judas had already left to commit his act of betrayal. Over the course of several hours, in the darkness of early morning, he was sorrowful to the point of death. *And being in agony, he prayed more earnestly. Then his sweat became like great drops of blood falling down to the ground* (Luke 22:44).

Jesus, the Son of God but also a human being, wrestled with what lay before him. As he completely yielded his will to the will of the Father, drops of blood fell from his face to the ground. The beginning of the blood sacrifice would start in the garden. This was only the beginning of the blood he would shed as the Lamb of God who willingly yielded his life as a sacrifice. Three times Jesus appealed to his Father, *if it is possible, let this* **cup** *pass from me.* And three times the Father said no.

Brian imagined the conversation:

"FATHER, IS THERE ANY OTHER WAY? DO I HAVE TO GO THROUGH WITH THIS?"

"SON, DO YOU LOVE THEM?"

"YES FATHER, I DO LOVE THEM. THEY ARE MY FRIENDS AND I DON'T WANT TO LOSE THEM."

"THEN THERE IS NO OTHER WAY. ALL RIGHTEOUSNESS MUST BE FULFILLED. THERE CAN BE NO MERCY WITHOUT JUDGEMENT AND THERE CAN BE NO GRACE WITHOUT JUSTICE."

"YES FATHER, I KNOW YOU ARE RIGHT. I WILL DO WHAT NEEDS TO BE DONE."

Somewhere in Brian's imaginary conversation between Jesus and the Father, he discovered a central truth. "THERE CAN BE NO MERCY WITHOUT JUDGEMENT AND THERE CAN BE NO GRACE WITHOUT JUSTICE." He kept mulling this over in his mind. How did this relate to the cup?

Then Brian understood. The cup that Jesus had to drink was the cup of his Father's judgment and wrath. Brian caught his breath and could barely comprehend this realization. The Father, who loved his beloved son, his only son, was willing to sacrifice him like a slaughtered lamb for the redemption of humanity. It was a divine agreement between Father and Son. Jesus, who loved his Father with infinite love, willingly allowed the judgment of his Father, reserved for a rebellious race of people, to fall upon himself instead of the ones who deserved it. Jesus endured it all so his friends and all who believe could be with him for eternity.

What love! What sacrifice! Brian struggled to understand. *Greater love has no one than this, than to lay down one's life for his friends* (John 15:13). All God ever wanted were friends who would love him and trust him. But because of the deception of Satan, fear and doubt entered the heart of man towards his maker. Satan continues to whisper lies leading to doubt, as he did in the garden, "did God really say...?" The redemption of mankind was possible, but God would have to do it for them. In the process, the Father would demonstrate an incomprehensible love and win back the hearts and minds of the people he created with the free will to choose. *But God demonstrates his own love for us in this: While we were still sinners, Christ died for us* (Romans 5:8).

God's perfect justice was satisfied through the obedience of his own Son unto death, thereby providing the blood sacrifice demanded by God's law allowing for mercy to be extended to all who accept and receive God's pardon offered to all who believe. *For the wages of sin is death, but the gift of God is eternal life in Christ Jesus our Lord* (Romans 6:23).

Brian imagined what was in the metaphorical cup that Jesus drank. A cup so vile and so disgusting we would never get near it as the stench would be unbearable. You couldn't be in the same room with it! Yet he drank this cup of God's wrath so we could drink the from the cup of salvation. To understand the cup is to understand what was accomplished and what it cost. Never again would Brian partake in Communion the same way. In fact, it had been years since he even participated in Communion and was looking forward to Sunday with great anticipation.

Chapter 20:

Nature Beckons

It was Friday. Brian checked online and found out his next flight was moved back to Monday but would still be on call for Sunday if the need arose. There would be a four-hour window if Crew Scheduling called, a window of time long enough to check out a church in the area.

Brian had grown up Baptist, but fresh with new revelation from studying the "cup," he was compelled to visit where they served Communion. Only a few churches offered the sacrament every Sunday. Not being Catholic, that was out. A little research and Brian found there were several churches that could work. Not knowing the differences in the various denominations, he was hoping for a fellowship that was not affiliated. Checking out local churches online, he saw that the website for Bread of Life Community Church said they celebrate weekly communion. What a name! "Bread of Life" was perfect. That's where they would go when Sunday arrived.

Maryanne returned home around half past noon with a bag of groceries. "Are you still in your bathrobe?" she chided. Brian didn't even realize it. He had been consumed all morning with study and church hunting.

197

"It's not like I had anywhere to go. I got engrossed in my new books." Brian knew Maryanne was agitated. He slipped out to the garage to grab the rest of the groceries. "How was the gym?" Brian tried to get the conversation flowing.

"It was good." Maryanne was not being very talkative. This may take a little work.

"Did you see anyone you know?"

"I saw Lucy at the grocery store." She was a neighbor from down the street. "It was her day off. We chatted for a few minutes. Her daughter, Renee, is not doing so well in school and may have to get a math tutor. I don't know how she's going to afford one."

As soon as Maryanne started talking about other people, he was home free. She wasn't talking about him! "That's too bad. I'm glad Hyler is good in math, thanks to your constant help."

"Yeah, being a single mom is a tough road. Everyone suffers. Lucy must work long hours just to make ends meet, which leaves Renee to fend for herself after school. I really feel bad for both of them." Maryanne said sadly.

"Is there anything we can do to help? Could Renee come over here after school and work on her math with Hyler?" Brian asked.

This was a new challenge. Usually, the conversation would be about someone but never so far as to try to help. The idea of self-sacrifice did not come easy to either of them. Brian knew it was the right thing to ask.

"You know, maybe we could help them. Why not? I will give her a call tonight." Maryanne smiled. She liked the idea of helping someone. It felt good.

Brian smiled as well. It was a step in the direction of service. After everything he'd read that morning about what God did for man, the least they could do was help a neighbor in need.

The phone rang. Maryanne answered. "Oh, hi. Yes, that will be fine, I can be there. Okay, see you then."

"Who was that?"

"It was the school. They want me at the front office to help again. One of their volunteers couldn't make it. I need to be there at 1:30. Does that work for you?"

"Sure, that's fine. Where would you like to go for dinner?"

"You choose. I should be back by 4:00."

They shared a quick sandwich for lunch and Brian was alone again until Hyler got home at 3:30. Study time was over. Jaunting upstairs, it was past time to get dressed. A beautiful May afternoon was calling, and he wasn't going to waste it. Peachtree City is a model of what suburban life should be like. No ugly strip malls in this town! As a planned community established in 1959, around 20% of the original 12,000 acres of land was off limits to development and were designated as greenbelt areas. As the airport grew, so did the city, and gradually morphed into a bedroom community for Delta Airlines. With great schools and minimal crime, it was locally known as "the bubble."

Brian had at least two hours before Hyler got home. The woods were beckoning. Folding the golf cart windshield down and flipping the lever to reverse gear, a high-pitched buzz let the whole neighborhood know someone was backing out. The warm wind in his face felt wonderful and thought about the old proverb, "Take time to smell the roses." We go through life at a breakneck speed, from one distraction to the next, and miss the glory of God's creation all around us. This was certainly true for him and was taking that old proverb to heart.

Brian guided the electric cart as it quietly traversed the trails towards his destination. With surrounding houses barely visible behind the trees, one might think they were in the middle of a deep forest. After a couple miles, he pulled into the nature preserve behind the community amphitheater. A long boardwalk jutted into the middle of the wetlands. Only one other golf cart was parked.

Brian walked slowly out into the preserve covered with trees like a giant canopy and leaned against the railing to take in the scenery. In the stillness of the preserve, nothing was moving. He looked closer. Still nothing. Looking even closer, a caterpillar was climbing slowly up a tree. Ants in a line were marching somewhere, traveling back and forth carrying their heavy loads. Bees were buzzing around the multi-colored wildflowers proudly displaying their beauty. Suddenly, a squirrel jumped from one branch to another and then a second squirrel took up the chase. They scurried up and down the trees, playing tag. A black-capped chickadee landed about five feet from him on the railing, turned its head a few times and flew off to find a new perch.

At first glance, he had seen nothing. Upon closer inspection, he realized that life was buzzing, running, crawling, and flying all around him. The minutes flew by; it was time to head back. He was thankful and happy just knowing that the infinite Creator of the universe is the author of life, not death. Brian came to understand that death was an aberration, and God was in the process of restoring the world back to its original glory, before the fall of Adam, when death was unthinkable.

It felt like he was caught up in the middle of a story that had been playing out for a long time with an arch villain and a superhero who saved those who had come under the villain's evil control. The spell of unbelief was broken for Brian. Would the chalice be used to help others escape the spell? Brian wondered where it was all leading.

Chapter 21:

Sunday

The weekend was a blur. Dinner Friday night at a popular restaurant... a dance lesson for Hyler Saturday morning... yard work in the afternoon and dinner with friends from the club that night. It is amazing how a busy schedule can crowd out thoughts that might soar to a higher level if allowed. It explains why God commanded the Sabbath, a day when people are supposed to rest and focus on him. Otherwise, we would probably crowd out all our days with activity of one kind or another, which is what Brian used to do, but not anymore. Brian was amazed at how his priorities continued to change, not in a forced way, but as a natural outgrowth of his new identity in Christ.

Sunday dawned and Brian awoke with a sense of exhilaration and expectation. Church may be mundane for many, but he felt like a kid about to go to a spiritual amusement park for the first time. No explanation would suffice. It was a genuine need to connect with God in a corporate setting... to hear the words, sing the songs, but most of all, to receive Communion and worship the God who filled his once dirty and empty cup.

He told Maryanne what church he wanted to visit. Being a close-knit airline community; they would probably know a few people who attended, at least that was the hope. Brian looked online and found out they offered a contemporary service where casual dress was the norm. He liked that idea. It was less intimidating, especially for Maryanne. Women always worry about what to wear, and whether someone might be wearing the same thing. *Oh, the horror!* Brian smiled at the thought.

A greeter met them at the door and made them feel welcome. They found seats in the back to be a little more anonymous, while praise music played in the background and people got settled. The band, complete with drums, guitars, a keyboard, and three vocalists, took the platform. A worship leader engaged the congregation and invited everyone to stand and sing. Brian only remembered a few Baptist hymns from high school, but the music was upbeat with simple lyrics projected onto a screen. Hyler was clapping in time with others around them. Maryanne was more reserved. Brian took it all in and allowed his spirit to soar with the corporate worship. Four songs later, the band was done. They would play another song or two later in the service. Everyone sat down.

Pastor Jack Smith, originally with the Lutheran church, was a man of average height, appeared to be in his early 60's with a tanned and ruddy complexion. His hair, light brown, was only slightly receding, but the grey was overtaking fast. He had a handshake of steel with the roughness of someone who worked the land. Brian would later find out he owned a small farm in the county and supplemented his income growing and selling landscape trees. His wife, Joanne, was a kindergarten teacher. Jack took the podium to give the invocation. He had a rich baritone voice and spoke like someone who knew how to communicate with an audience.

The service had a friendly contemporary feel but still contained many traditional elements borrowed from his past Lutheran affiliation. Brian followed along in the bulletin and recited the Apostles Creed. Encapsulated in a comprehensive set of statements, creeds summarize the core fundamentals of what Christians are supposed to believe, from the Holy Trinity to the virgin birth. Even though the atmosphere was casual, the order of worship was still structured. Brian liked it, as a pilot and an engineer, structure is a good thing.

The reading for the sermon was from the 73rd Psalm when the author was complaining to God about why good things happen to bad people when it seems good people often suffer.

After the reading by another member of the church, Pastor Jack took the podium again and began his sermon.

"The Psalm we just read is a Psalm of Asaph one of several writers of the Psalms besides David. Here he complains about how godless and evil people still seem to prosper in life. Hear again what he says…

But as for me, my feet had almost slipped; I had nearly lost my foothold. For I envied the arrogant when I saw the prosperity of the wicked.

"Asaph described the prosperity of the wicked, which offended his sense of fairness, as he was doing his best to live a moral life. Listen again to his description:

From their callous hearts comes iniquity and their evil imaginations have no limits. They scoff and speak with malice; with arrogance they threaten oppression. This is what the wicked are like always free of care, they go on amassing wealth.

"The apparent contradiction vexed him. He contemplated the purpose of living a moral life. Why bother when the wicked seem to prosper anyway?

Surely in vain I have kept my heart pure and have washed my hands in innocence. All day long I have been afflicted, and every morning brings new punishments.

"Asaph then gains a different perspective, from the vantage point of eternity. See how the Psalm transitions.

When I tried to understand all this, it troubled me deeply till I entered the sanctuary of God; then I understood their final destiny.

"Asaph ends his Psalm recognizing that the pleasures of the godless are short lived. He knew that living a life of faith and integrity was not a waste of time simply because bad people have fleeting success. He realized the promise of eternity was his, and says, *my flesh and my heart may fail, but God is the strength of my heart and my portion forever.*

"However, a more pressing question for many is why there is suffering and evil in the first place and why good people are allowed to suffer. Here are some common explanations.

"Some say it is because we live in a fallen world.

"Some say it is because the world is filled with sin which carries inevitable consequences.

"Some say even though God loves us, he does not remove the consequences for bad behavior and bad decisions.

"Some say it is because we have an adversary called Satan who, because we belong to God, seeks our harm. Although that is true, can we really blame everything on him?

"There must be more of an answer to this perplexing question.

"Christianity teaches that God is loving and good, but can we make this claim in the face of suffering and evil? Some people use these negative realities as an argument against the existence of God.

"Of the many reasons people often give for rejecting Christianity, the problem of suffering is the most difficult to deal with because it is so personal. All of us have suffered in this life, all of us have been affected by evil and many have questioned God's goodness in the face of suffering. The fact that people suffer may not be a strong argument against the existence of God, but it may be an argument against a *loving* God.

"This single question is perhaps the biggest stumbling block to faith. However, if the Son of God suffered more than most of us will ever be called to endure by experiencing the extreme agony of crucifixion, and if he did it on our behalf, then that changes the equation.

"We still can't explain the great tragedies in life and perhaps we never will. Nevertheless, in Jesus Christ, we can find spiritual strength to face suffering and evil with hope and courage rather than bitterness and despair. Paul writes in Philippians 4:13, *I can do all things through Christ who strengthens me.* That same strength is offered to every believer.

"What is the source of that strength? It is the power of the cross and the resurrection. Christ's willingness to endure the cross lets us know in the most dramatic way possible that God truly cares for us. The cross means we never have to doubt the love of God. But it didn't stop with the grave. The resurrection offers assurance that suffering and evil will one day come to an end. God's ministry to us is past, present, and future. The cross blots out our sinful past while the resurrection gives us hope for an eternal future. And in the now, in the present, we have the truth and comfort of God's word and the guidance of his Spirit.

"Our suffering today is only temporary. Through suffering, pain, and hardships, God is able to build character, strength, and endurance that would never have developed otherwise. God doesn't cause our suffering but uses it to strengthen us if we allow him. What God can achieve through our pain is up to us.

"As Jesus said to his disciples in John 16:33, *Be of good cheer, I have overcome the world.* This is the promise of your faith: You too have overcome the world. Put everything in the context of eternity as Asaph did in the 73rd Psalm and remember what Paul wrote in Romans 8:18, *I consider that our present sufferings are not worth comparing with the glory that will be revealed in us. Amen.*

Communion

Brian thought of Tom Jennings and some of the objections he raised. He reflected on Jim Covino from the Air Force, how he was suffering the agony of divorce. There were so many that needed to hear how much God loves them, that they are not alone in this world.

They had come to the part of the service he longed for the most. It would be his first Communion since high school. The church of his youth, for some reason, only celebrated this Sacrament once a quarter. That didn't seem to be often enough... not anymore.

Pastor Jack walked down from the podium to the Communion table. Catholics call it the altar. On either side of the table was a long prayer bench where some people kneel to pray after receiving Communion. The elements of bread and juice were ready. The pastor held up the bread and said, "As the Apostle Paul instructed almost 2,000 years ago, *For I received from the Lord what I also passed on to you: The Lord Jesus, on the night he was betrayed, took bread, and when he had given thanks, he broke it and said, 'This is my body, which is broken for you; do this in remembrance of me* (1 Cor 11:23-24). The minister broke the load of bread and placed it back on the table.

He then took the juice and poured it from a pitcher into a large goblet and said, *In the same way, after supper he took the cup, saying, 'This cup is the new covenant in my blood; do this, whenever you drink it, in remembrance of me.' For whenever you eat this bread and drink this cup, you proclaim the Lord's death until he comes* (1 Cor 11:25-26).

The minister placed the goblet on the table. He explained to the guests how it would be done. Each row, starting from the front, would come forward. There were two sets of elders on either side of the table for two stations to serve both sides of the church. The first elder would offer the loaf, and the participant would break off a piece. The elder would say, "Body of Christ, broken for you." The next station was the juice. The participant would take the bread and dip it in the goblet. The elder would say, "Blood of Christ, shed for you." This very real symbol of the body and blood of Christ would be consumed as the participant walked back to his or her seat. The pastor explained how this method of Communion was called "intinction," where the bread would be dipped into the wine or juice. Any believer in Christ who wasn't living in a lifestyle of sin was welcome to participate, including children over the age of six.

It was time for their row to go down. Brian was in great anticipation and held Hyler's hand. Maryanne decided not to go and stayed back in the row to observe. It didn't seem right for her to participate. She was moved by the sermon and the music, but wasn't quite ready to commit. That was okay with Brian. He didn't want to push her.

"Will this be like the fountain of living water?" Hyler asked.

"Hyler, communion is how we remember the event that allows us to have the living water. If Jesus didn't die, then we couldn't live forever with him in heaven." Hyler just smiled and was eager to receive the elements with her dad.

It wasn't a mystery for Hyler. Simple faith is a gift. Brian was still confused over the doctrinal differences within Christianity. He put all the debate aside and would receive the elements in faith, just like Hyler. That was enough.

Hyler went first. She broke the bread, dipped it in the juice and ate it slowly as if to savor its flavor. It wasn't the best thing she ever tasted, but maybe the most important. Brian was next. Breaking a piece from the loaf, he remembered Jesus' agony in the Garden of Gethsemane. Moving to the elder holding the goblet, he dipped the bread in the juice which was immediately soaked in red. Brian remembered the drops of blood mixed with sweat in the Garden of Gethsemane as Jesus travailed over what he was about to endure. He consumed the elements, turned toward the prayer bench and kneeled as others had done. With eyes closed for a moment, he prayed, "Thank you, Lord, for your extreme love as demonstrated by such an extreme sacrifice. Thank you for coming into my life, and Hyler too. Please help Maryanne believe."

Rising from the bench, he made his way back to where Maryanne was sitting. She was moved by his sincerity. *This was real for him, and Hyler seemed so peaceful*, she thought. Like peering into an old attic, or opening a long-locked closet, God was clearing out the cobwebs of doubt and unbelief.

They met Pastor Jack. "Pastor, I really enjoyed your message."

"Thank you and thanks for coming. Come back and see us."

"I think we will," Brian said with a broad smile.

Brian and Maryanne greeted a few other people they recognized. As they headed to the parking lot, Brian asked, "What do you guys want for lunch?"

"A Happy Meal!" Hyler chimed.

"Under one condition." Brian said as he held her hand. "That we make it a picnic. Are you ok with that dear?" he asked looking at Maryanne.

McDonalds was not on the top of her list. "Sure, but can you and I split a sub sandwich instead?"

"Not a problem, we just make two quick stops instead of one."

They picked up their food and drove over to Lake Peachtree where a small park was waiting with several shaded picnic tables. Brian liked the spot; it offered a panoramic view and there were always ducks and geese to feed. Hyler loved luring the geese over to snatch the bread right out of her hand.

It was a wonderful, relaxing afternoon. Brian didn't say much about church. He didn't want to press the issue. He knew Maryanne needed to come to faith at her own pace. The last thing he wanted was for Christianity to become a dividing line in their relationship.

Brian walked by himself out onto the fishing dock while Mom and Daughter continued to feed the friendly fowl with scraps from their lunch. He whispered another prayer. "Lord, I need Maryanne with me in this new walk. I can't do it alone. Speak to her spirit and prepare her heart. Help her to receive you, Lord. Amen."

The rest of the day was lazy. Hyler had homework to do. Brian went to the golfing range, though his heart wasn't in it. He stood there hitting little white balls with a graphite stick and wondered if this was the best use of his time. Right then, happiness would be found digging into a book that might offer more insight into his transformed life. Brian packed up his clubs and went home. Maryanne was planning an early dinner anyway.

After the meal, Brian helped with the dishes again. Trying to keep things positive, he wanted no barriers to what God might do next.

Maryanne was rather quiet most of the day and immersed in her own thoughts. She enjoyed their picnic with the ducks and appreciated church too. Even though she grew up Methodist, it just never clicked. She too had collected a basket full of objections over the years. Her mother died of breast cancer when she was a sophomore in college. It was devastating and was the real reason she dropped out of school. She prayed like everyone else in that situation and wondered why God never showed up. Hyler was a blessing, but was a miscarriage really necessary with no prospect of any more children? These and other realities had left a bitterness towards God and religion. Christmas and Easter were all she could handle and even that was for Hyler.

But something was changing in her heart and mind. The sermon hit a chord she needed to hear. Maybe it was everything put together; the music, the prayers, the creed but what moved her most was the apparent impact of this newfound faith on Brian. *It is real to him; maybe it is real after all*, she thought.

God was hard at work preparing another heart to receive him. As Hyler's bedtime approached, Brian asked Maryanne if they could all read a Bible story together. Maryanne was agreeable and even found herself eager to hear the story. Hyler picked out the same one as the night Brian got home from Rome. Kids love repetition. It was The Woman at the Well. As she finished the story, Hyler asked her mother, "Don't you want to have the living water too, mom?"

Maryanne's eyes welled up with tears. She was ready. "Yes… I do, Hyler. Will you help me?"

"Dad and I will both help you. Just ask Jesus into your heart! It's easy."

Brian knew it was never easy for an adult. They have too many questions, objections and habits they are afraid might need to be given up. People don't realize that God helps in the process, like an alcoholic suddenly losing the desire to drink. She was about to make a U-turn and give faith a chance. She asked Jesus into her life with Brian and Hyler flanking her on the bed. They all hugged in a huddle. Brian whispered a prayer and thanked God for transforming his family. It was a blessing beyond Brian's comprehension.

Chapter 22:

The Dream

Sunday night felt like Christmas morning. Maryanne had a joy in her heart she had never experienced before. All the questions and objections she might have raised were no longer an issue. She had a feeling of tranquility and peace. There was a knowing of God's presence that was more than just an intellectual acknowledgment. Jesus had become real. Maryanne moved from a conceptual understanding of God to knowing his presence in her soul. What a difference! She could sense it, but could never explain it, yet it was new, real and wonderful.

Brian and Maryanne were like kids getting ready for bed, cutting jokes and laughing. The couple hadn't been this lighthearted in years. In bed, they hugged each other with a love that was more intense than either one had ever felt. It was emanating from a source that was deep and pure. Like newlyweds, they fell asleep in each other's arms.

At about three o'clock in the morning, Brian began to stir and shifted to be lying on his back. Still asleep, his eyes started to move rapidly and was drawn into a dream he would remember for the rest of his life.

Brian was back in Orvieto and was walking into the well. All three of the women he had met in Italy were waiting, dressed in white robes. Sarah, Maria, and Emanuella were all smiling and motioning to go into the well. Sarah called out as he descended, "Brian, you must trust me. You will die at the bottom, but you will live at the top. The world says you must live before you die. The truth is you must die before you can live. Do you trust me?"

Brian called out in his real voice, "Yes, I trust you!" Maryanne woke up for a second and went back to sleep.

Brian felt no fear. He continued to descend into the well and noticed his clothes were filthy. His shirt had stains all over it and so did his pants. His hands were dirty with crud all under the fingernails, even his shoes looked like they were caked with mud and couldn't understand why he was so unsightly.

Halfway down, he saw himself praying with Sarah standing a few feet away, just like it had happened a few days earlier. Farther down, he saw himself kneeling on the platform, praying and praising God, the same way it happened. Then the image changed to something new. He was no longer observing himself as though he was another person but felt himself lying on the platform motionless and covered in blood. Like an after-death experience, he saw himself leave his body. He was conscious of himself but separated from his body which was lying motionless on the platform. He turned and started to climb the stairs with a sudden realization that he was no longer filthy; in fact, he was dressed in a white robe– the same as the women-and continued to ascend the stairs. Emerging from the entrance, he looked for the women, but they were gone. Brian started walking in the direction of Pacella's just like the first time.

With a natural height of about six feet, he felt much higher and noticed he was carrying Sarah's Bible in his right hand and the paper cup in his left. As Brian continued to walk, people looked at him with astonishment. Was it the ankle length white robe? He looked down at his hands, the Bible had become a knife. A few minutes later, he glanced down again, and it had grown to a dagger. The third time, he stopped and stared. The dagger had become a sword, and he realized his entire demeanor and appearance had changed. He was holding The Chalice of Truth in his left hand and a sword in his right. The robe had vanished and he was wearing the armaments of a medieval knight. A helmet covered his head, the chest area was protected by a brass plate, his boots were made of bronze, and a large belt wrapped around his waist. A circular shield was hooked onto the belt allowing his left arm to be free with which he held the chalice. The sword was razor sharp and shimmered with light that emanated from the blade like an electrical charge, moving back and forth along both edges.

Suddenly, Brian was no longer in Orvieto but rather in America. He didn't recognize the city, but was in a park surrounded by hundreds of people and appeared to be about twelve feet tall. His voice thundered. While holding the chalice up at an angle, water cascaded out of it like a fountain. People came to the water by hundreds and thousands. They were thirsty and appeared to have been dragged in out of the desert or out of some catastrophe. Some were drinking with both hands, some were bathing in it like a shower, and others were rolling in it. They all joyfully drank and experienced the water. Even though there were thousands rushing to get a taste of the water, there was always room for more to gather.

On his right side, people were hurling insults at him and cursing him. Their lips were drawn up into a snarl as they spewed their hate. Brian pointed the sword at them and said only one thing: REPENT OR PERISH, THE TIME FOR DECISION IS NOW. As he pointed the sword, it became a blade of brilliant light and instantly extended piercing the heart and then immediately retracted. The angry soul collapsed to the ground and would either crawl in tears toward the water falling from the chalice or rise with hatred and run into the shadows. The choice was theirs to make.

Brian peered into the darkness to see what was lurking and could make out the forms and shapes of creatures that looked like some sort of half-man, half-rodent hybrid. They were vile and disgusting. Every few minutes, one ventured out of the shadows and ran toward Brian, and he commanded with a voice that sounded like God: YOU HAD YOUR CHANCE! YOU MADE YOUR DECISION! YOU SIDED WITH THE ENEMY OF ALL HEAVEN AND I BIND YOU NOW TO THE PIT, WHICH IS YOUR ETERNAL DESTINY IN THE NAME OF JESUS, THE ALMIGHTY CHRIST OF GOD AND SAVIOR OF MANKIND. The sword shot out, like before, and the creature suddenly vanished from sight.

This went on for what seemed to be days, maybe even weeks, until suddenly thick clouds gathered overhead. The buildings surrounding the park began to collapse. The number of people who came to drink dwindled to nothing. The water stopped flowing from the chalice. As darkness encroached, all that was left were the hordes of the lost gathering around him. Their clothes were filthy and vile, and their eyes were filled with the blackness of evil with mouths like open sewers spewing nothing but excrement. Mixed in with the gathering horde were the creatures.

Brian had no fear. Instantly his armament was gone. The sword once again became Sarah's Bible, the paper cup was back in his left hand, and he was again dressed in a dazzling white robe. As he gazed up into the sky, the gathering clouds parted. As the horde was about to overtake him, Brian ascended out of their midst into the sky. The earth came into view below and for what seemed to be only a few seconds, he saw nothing but light. The next thing that came into view was an enormous celestial city that glittered like gold, illuminated from within. It was more beautiful than anyone could ever describe. Millions of other white-robed saints were arriving at the same time. He was home.

Chapter 23:

The Interpretation

Brian woke up. It was five o'clock in the morning. He remembered everything. This was no ordinary dream. Was this a vision? Maryanne was still sleeping. He slipped down into the den, turned on his laptop, and typed everything out. He didn't want to forget even the smallest detail; this dream meant something.

Pulling out Sarah's business card, he sent her an email. It read:

Sarah,

It was so good meeting you in Orvieto. Because of you my life will never be the same. Thank you for giving me your Bible. It means more than you can ever know. Now I have a favor to ask of you. I just woke up from a vivid dream. I think it was a vision. I have attached a Word document describing what was in the dream. Nothing was left out. Would you please take a stab at interpreting this for me? You were right on the money when we met in the well. I think you will know what all of this means. Thanks for your help.

Brian Michaels

Sarah was sitting at her office computer when the message came in. It was not quite noon on Monday in Rome. Looking at her schedule, she saw that the afternoon appointment had already been moved to another day. After printing out his email with the attachments, she left the office for her apartment. The timing was good; it was lunch hour. As a senior sales rep she was the master of her own schedule. Sarah was happy to get Brian's note and had wondered when he would reach out. *God is really working on him*, she thought. There was a second document attached describing the chalice and his experience in the well after she left him. Heeding the wisdom of an old proverb—that a faded note is better than the sharpest memory—Brian had taken the time to write it all down over the previous two nights.

Sarah sat on the bed and began to read. Stunned by what happened to him after they parted company, Brian's description of The Chalice of Truth made her wish he could have been there to meet Father Gabelli! Next Sarah read Brian's recounting of the dream. Awestruck by the message, her deep knowledge of Scripture allowed her to know exactly what it meant. It would take time to explain. Opening an online Bible App called Bible Gateway on her computer, the first thing she needed to do was track down all the relevant verses. She was excited to have such an important assignment and wrote a quick note back to Brian:

Brian,

Thanks for your note. It was wonderful meeting you too. Wow, it seems like God has got you on a fast track to something important. These things don't just happen. I printed out both of your attachments and already have some thoughts on your dream, but I need to confirm everything with the Word before I can respond. I will begin to work on it now. I hope to have something for you tonight.

Blessings to you and your family,

Sarah Foxworth

Brian was sitting at the computer waiting and hoping for a response. Fantastic! She would have an answer that night. Then Brian thought about work. The flight to Barcelona left around 6:00 PM. During Daylight Savings Time in Atlanta, it would be 11:00 PM in Rome. Would she be able to send the explanation before he had to leave for the airport at 4:00? Brian was hoping… and praying.

Sarah started to dig. She took the dream description paragraph by paragraph to find the Scriptural applications. It was her contention that if she couldn't find where it lined up with the Word, then it was just a dream and not from God.

She decided to break it down even further into separate scenes since a single paragraph may contain multiple ideas. Each scene may have its own significance. She took the paper and drew lines across each paragraph where a new thought needed to be clarified. Good gracious! There were 15 different scenes! This dream was important; it was meant to communicate something specific and imminent. Sarah had to work hard and fast–a sense of urgency arose in her spirit. There was no time to waste.

Sarah was accustomed to preparing complex proposals. Her research was always thorough and well planned. She opened a new Word document and constructed a memo offering a description and detailed analysis of Brian's dream.

Sarah's Memo

For others who may read this document, the following is a Scriptural interpretation of a dream/vision received by Brain Michaels. For the purposes of clarity:

- The dream description is in **bold.**

- The Scripture is in *italics.*

- My comments are in regular text.

- It is broken into fifteen separate ideas.

I was back in Orvieto and was walking into the well. All three of the women I had met in Italy were waiting for me, dressed in white robes. Sarah, Maria and Emanuella were all smiling and motioning me to go into the well.

The key image here is the white robes. From your story of the chalice, all three of the women you met are believers in Christ. The white robes represent the righteousness of Christ that now belongs to the believer. You were seeing them in the spirit, as God sees them.

For he has clothed me with garments of salvation and arrayed me in a robe of righteousness (Isaiah 61:10).

Sarah called out to me as I descended, "Brian, you must trust me. You will die at the bottom, but you will live at the top. The world says you must live before you die. The truth is you must die before you can live. Do you trust me?" I called out, "Yes, I trust you!"

There are a couple of concepts here. The first is trust. We must trust in God's love even though we don't know where he is leading us. In your dream, I must have represented God or an angel because I spoke the Word of God to you in the well. You affirmed your faith by saying, "I trust you."

The next concept is dying to self. The Kingdom of God is like a mirror image of our world, what is left is right, what is right is left. Think of it. Jesus says that if we give, it will be given back with greater measure. The world would say if you gave less you get to keep more for yourself. Jesus says that we are to love our enemies. The world wants to hate its enemies. Jesus says to do good to those who do you wrong. The world wants to retaliate. We must learn the principles of God's Kingdom. They are the opposite of what comes naturally.

The man who loves his life will lose it, while the man who hates his life in this world will keep it for eternity (John 12:25-26).

In the same way, count yourselves dead to sin but alive to God in Christ Jesus (Romans 6:11).

These are two verses of many that talk about not following the former lusts and desires of your old life–before you asked Christ into your heart. The old man is dead; a new man–a spiritual man–has been born. That is who you are. You are no longer the old man. You must come to understand your new identity in Christ as a redeemed son of the living God, an heir to his kingdom!

I felt no fear. I continued my descent into the well and noticed my clothes were filthy. My shirt had stains all over it and so did my pants. Even my hands were dirty with crud all under the fingernails and my shoes looked

like they were caked with mud and didn't understand why I was so unsightly but continued down into the well.

You mentioned you had no fear. Even though what you saw might ordinarily be frightening, you were surrounded by the love of God.

There is no fear in love. But perfect love drives out fear, because fear has to do with punishment (1 John 4:18).

God was revealing something to you in this vision; however, you were never the target of judgment or condemnation.

Therefore, there is now no condemnation for those who are in Christ Jesus, because through Christ Jesus the law of the Spirit of life set me free from the law of sin and death (Romans 8:1-2).

You saw yourself as filthy because God wanted you to see how he sees those who are outside of Christ. All the filth and stain represent sin. People think they are perfectly fine yet have no concept of how they appear to God. Only Christ can free us from the law of sin and death. There is no one who is worthy of heaven apart from Christ.

All of us have become like one who is unclean, and all our righteous acts are like filthy rags (Isaiah 64:6).

This righteousness from God comes through faith in Jesus Christ to all who believe. There is no difference, for all have sinned and fall short of the glory of God (Romans 3:23).

Halfway down, I saw myself praying with Sarah standing a few feet away, just like it happened the other day. Farther down, I saw myself kneeling on the platform, praying and praising God, the same way it happened.

This is a sequence of events. God was showing how you entered the well covered and consumed with the sins of the world. You were just like everyone else whose lives are described as "filthy rags," even though they may think they are good. He revealed what happened when you gave your life to Christ–you were filled with his Spirit. You became a child of God.

Yet to all who received him, to those who believed in his name, he gave the right to become children of God (John 1:11-12).

Then the image changed to something new. I was no longer observing myself as though I was another person, but felt myself lying on the platform motionless and covered in blood.

This image represents your old self, dead to sin. By faith, you have been covered with the blood of Christ and that is what removes the stain of sin. It is what allows you to be filled with God's Spirit. God cannot fill a vessel that is also filled with sin. The sin must be removed, and only the blood of sacrifice has the power to do it.

Without the shedding of blood there is no forgiveness (Hebrews 9:22).

Like an after-death experience, I saw myself leave my body. I was conscious of myself and yet I saw my body motionless on the platform. I turned and started to climb the stairs.

The vision allowed you to see your old self dead on the platform. You have become a new creation. The spirit-man within is now alive with Christ. You saw your spirit-man rise from the flesh of the old man that is now dead.

As for you, you were dead in your transgressions and sins, in which you used to live when you followed the ways of this world and of the ruler of the kingdom of the air, the spirit who is now at work in those who are disobedient (Ephesians 2:1-3).

Suddenly I realized that I was no longer filthy; in fact, I was dressed in a white robe–the same as the women. I continued to ascend the stairs and emerged from the entrance. I looked for the women, but they were gone. I started walking in the direction of Pacella's just like the first time.

This confirms your salvation. You have been clothed with his righteousness and not your own. The robe represents the righteousness of God.

You are all sons of God through faith in Christ Jesus, for all of you who were baptized into Christ have clothed yourselves with Christ (Galatians 3:26-27).

I felt taller. My natural height is about six feet, but this was much higher.

Remember Goliath? He was a giant in the flesh and the Israelite army was afraid of him. Not David: he was small in stature but mighty in faith. So, when we are united with Christ, we can also become spiritual giants. That is what you were experiencing. Even the demons will flee from the presence of Christ within you.

I was carrying your Bible in my right hand and the paper cup in my left. As I continued to walk, people looked at me with astonishment. Was it the ankle length white robe? I looked down at my hands, the Bible had become a knife. After a few minutes, I glanced down again, and it had grown to a dagger. The third time, I stopped and stared. The dagger had become a sword.

This speaks to the progressive nature of the Christian walk. The Word of God is referred to as the "sword of the Spirit." As with any swordsman, skill comes with knowledge and practice. The image of the knife becoming a dagger and then becoming a sword was a sequence revealing how you will continue to grow in the Word. Your knowledge will eventually become like a sword in the hand of a warrior.

Take the... sword of the Spirit, which is the word of God (Ephesians 6:17).

For the word of God is living and active. Sharper than any double-edged sword, it penetrates even to dividing soul and spirit, joints and marrow; it judges the thoughts and attitudes of the heart (Hebrews 4:12-13).

I realized my entire demeanor and appearance had changed and I was holding The Chalice of Truth in my left hand and the sword in my right. The robe had vanished and I was wearing the armaments of a medieval knight. A helmet covered my head, the chest area was protected by a brass plate, my boots were made of bronze, and a large belt wrapped around my waist. A circular shield was hooked onto the belt allowing my left arm to be free with which I held the chalice. The sword was razor sharp and shimmered with light that emanated from the blade like an electrical charge, moving back and forth along both edges.

The vision shows you growing into spiritual maturity. It reveals how you were initially robed in the righteousness of Christ, but now you are called to be an active participant in the plan and purpose of God. To do this, you must be clothed in the armor of God. Paul writes in Ephesians how believers are to put on the 1) helmet of salvation, 2) the breast plate of righteousness, 3) the belt of truth, 4) the shield of faith, 5) shoes prepared to share the good news of salvation (the gospel), 6) and the sword of the Spirit, which is the Word of God. Why must we wear the armaments of a warrior? It is because Satan, the enemy of our souls, who was defeated by the cross of Christ, remains a force of opposition until he is completely vanquished when Christ returns at the end of the age. The believer must be prepared to defend his own faith and to fight the enemy on behalf of others still trapped in sin and unbelief.

For though we live in the world, we do not wage war as the world does. The weapons we fight with are not the weapons of the world. On the contrary, they have divine power to demolish strongholds (2 Corinthians 10:3-5).

The reason God has waited two thousand years to put an end to Satan is so that heaven can be filled with millions of souls from around the world who come into the kingdom through Christ. Many Jews are coming to Christ and are often called Messianic Jews, but most unfortunately will acknowledge Jesus as Messiah only after much suffering. Even though most Jews denied him initially, God's offer of salvation was extended to all, Jew and Gentile alike, through faith in Christ. There is not one way for Jews and another way for Gentiles. We all enter through the same door. We know the end of the age is at hand because of what God is doing with the Jews as a nation. After being scattered for twenty-five hundred years, they returned to Israel to become a nation in 1948 through the crucible of the holocaust. They regained complete control of Jerusalem in 1967. These are major fulfillments of end-time prophecy. It signals the end of "the time of the Gentiles," as described by Jesus. It indicates that God's two-thousand-year plan for the Church is ending, and he is turning his attention again to the Jews and their ultimate salvation.

Why has God waited so long to put an end to the enemy? When he destroys Satan in the lake of fire, he will also destroy sin. That will be the end and all those outside of Christ who will perish along with the devil and his horde of demons that plague the earth with evil. There will be no place to go but hell. Sin cannot dwell in the presence of holiness. God devised a different plan. Jesus would take our sins upon himself and allow all who believe to be clothed in his righteousness. This has been going on for two millennia and is called the Church Age. The greatest harvest of souls for the kingdom is about to happen. The following is a parable Jesus spoke about the end-time harvest.

"Where then did the weeds come from?"

"An enemy did this," he replied.

The servants asked him, "Do you want us to go and pull them up?"

"No," he answered, "because while you are pulling the weeds, you may root up the wheat with them. Let both grow together until the harvest. At that time I will tell the harvesters: First collect the weeds and tie them in bundles to be burned; then gather the wheat and bring it into my barn" (Matthew 13:24-30).

Suddenly, I was no longer in Orvieto but rather in America. I didn't recognize the city, but I was in a park surrounded by hundreds of people. It felt like I was about twelve feet tall. As I spoke, my voice thundered. I was holding the chalice up at an angle. Water cascaded out of it like a fountain. People came to drink the water by hundreds and thousands. They were thirsty and appeared to have been dragged in out of the desert or out of some catastrophe. Some were drinking with both hands, some were bathing in it like a shower, and others were rolling in it. They all drank the water joyfully. Even though there were hundreds, even thousands rushing to get a taste of the water, there was always room for more to gather.

This reveals that you will be an instrument of God's end-time harvest. You will be speaking words of life through the message of the Chalice of Truth. Remember what God told you at the bottom of the well? *"The water is my Word."* Water also symbolizes the Holy Spirit. You will be used to bring both the Word and the Spirit to a world desperate to hear the message of salvation. The Word is also cleansing, which is why in your dream, people were even bathing in it.

Christ loved the church and gave himself up for her to make her holy, cleansing her by the washing with water through the word, and to present her to himself as a radiant church, without stain or wrinkle or any other blemish, but holy and blameless (Ephesians 5:25-28).

We are cleansed and washed and sustained through the Word. The Word and God's Spirit cannot be separated; they work in unison. *The words I have spoken to you are spirit and they are life* (John 6:63).

On my right side, people were hurling insults and cursing at me. Their lips were drawn up into a snarl as they spewed their hate. I pointed the sword at them and said only one thing: REPENT OR PERISH, THE TIME FOR DECISION IS NOW. As I pointed the sword, it became a blade of brilliant light and instantly extended out piercing the heart and then immediately retracted. The angry soul collapsed to the ground and would either crawl in tears toward the water falling from the chalice or rise with

hatred and run back into the shadows. The choice was theirs to make.

Remember the parable of the harvest just above? Who are the wheat and weeds? This is a powerful metaphor. Remember Jesus' first miracle, the changing of water into wine? All of us were nothing more than weeds at one time, useless to a farmer and useless to God, who in most parables is seen as the owner of the farm, vineyard or orchard depending on the parable. We have been transformed from weeds to wheat just like Jesus changed water to wine. All those who reject Christ will be bundled up and cast into hell with Satan. Those who come to Christ are transformed by faith into something God can use. The picture of wheat and weeds is important. From a distance, they look the same. It is only upon closer inspection that you can tell the difference. One is useless, but the other can be turned into bread. Jesus calls himself the "bread of life" for all who believe. The great sadness is that Jesus rejects no one. People condemn themselves by their refusal to acknowledge their need of forgiveness and transformation through Christ.

I peered into the darkness to see what was lurking and could make out the forms and shapes of creatures that looked like some sort of half-man, half-rodent hybrid. They were vile and disgusting. Every few minutes, one ventured out of the shadows and ran toward me, and I

commanded with a voice that sounded like God: YOU HAD YOUR CHANCE! YOU MADE YOUR DECISION! YOU SIDED WITH THE ENEMY OF ALL HEAVEN AND I BIND YOU NOW TO THE PIT, WHICH IS YOUR ETERNAL DESTINY IN THE NAME OF JESUS, THE ALMIGHTY CHRIST OF GOD AND SAVIOR OF MANKIND. **The sword shot out, like before, and the creature suddenly vanished from sight.**

Brian, God is going to empower you with incredible boldness. You will be involved in much spiritual warfare. The vision reveals the enemy will not be happy with your success in stealing souls from the clutches of hell. God will give you great authority in his name over the demonic realm. He has given you this authority for one reason only–so you can win more souls for the kingdom before it is too late.

I have given you authority to trample on snakes and scorpions and to overcome all the power of the enemy; nothing will harm you. However, do not rejoice that the spirits submit to you, but rejoice that your names are written in heaven (Luke 10:19-20).

This went on for what seemed to be days, maybe even weeks. Suddenly, thick clouds gathered overhead. The buildings surrounding the park began to collapse. The number of people coming to drink from the chalice dwindled to nothing. The water stopped flowing from the chalice. All that was left were the hordes of the lost

239

gathering around me. Their clothes were filthy and vile, and their eyes were filled with the blackness of evil with mouths like open sewers spewing nothing but excrement. Mixed in with the gathering horde were the creatures.

As the end of the age approaches, there will be a worldwide revival. Millions will come to Christ. You will be part of that revival. With every day that passes, the world moves closer to financial collapse. Anarchy, war, terror, famine, epidemics, earthquakes, volcanoes and wicked weather will characterize the "birth pangs" leading up to the Great Tribulation of the end times. God must shake everything to the point of collapse in order to wake men and women out of their complacency. They must turn to Christ or perish. During this time of shaking, millions will turn to the Lord. Millions more will turn away. The demons of hell with Satan as their leader will be in the midst, blinding their eyes and hearts to the truth. Once blinded, they become filled with every vile sin and perversion. Their willful rejection of Christ will doom them to outer darkness and hell. The full measure of those who can be saved will eventually be achieved and then the end will come.

See to it that you do not refuse him who speaks. If they did not escape when they refused him who warned them on earth (Moses), how much less will we, if we turn away from him who warns us from heaven (Jesus)? At that time his voice shook the earth, but now he has promised, "Once more I will shake not only the earth but also the heavens" (Hebrews 12:25-26).

Through all of it, I did not fear. Suddenly, my armament was gone. The sword once again became your Bible, the paper cup was back in my left hand, and I was again dressed in a dazzling white robe. As I gazed up into the sky, the gathering clouds parted. As the horde was about to overtake me, I ascended out of their midst into the sky through the clouds that had just parted. The earth came into view below me and for what seemed to be only a few seconds, I saw nothing but light. The next thing that came into view was an enormous celestial city that glittered like gold, illuminated from within. It was more beautiful than anyone could ever describe. Millions of white-robed saints were arriving at the same time. I knew this was home.

Brian, what you have described is the end time "catching away" of the church. Some call this future event the "gathering together" of believers at the end. Evangelicals may call it "the rapture." They are different names for the same event. Satan and all those who rejected Christ will be judged and cast into hell. The total sum of all believers is called the Church and is also called the Bride of Christ. Jesus is the bridegroom. The removal of the Church at the time of the end is the bridegroom coming *as a thief in the night* to steal his bride away to the Father's house. The sequence of events follows exactly that of a Jewish wedding ceremony. The book of Revelation talks about all believers attending *The Marriage Supper of the Lamb*. The Church is removed because believers *have not been appointed unto wrath*. This is why you had no fear. You knew God was in control and you were not the object of his anger. Your vision reveals how God's removal of the Church will be at the last minute, when judgment begins here on earth.

Two key verses for this event are as follows:

Listen, I tell you a mystery: We will not all sleep, but we will all be changed–in a flash, in the twinkling of an eye, at the last trumpet. For the trumpet will sound, the dead will be raised imperishable, and we will be changed. For the perishable must clothe itself with the imperishable, and the mortal with immortality (1 Corinthians 15:51-54).

For the Lord himself will come down from heaven, with a loud command, with the voice of the archangel and with the trumpet call of God, and the dead in Christ will rise first. After that, we who are still alive and are left will be caught up together with them in the clouds to meet the Lord in the air. And so we will be with the Lord forever (1 Thessalonians 4:16).

Brian, your incredible vision takes you all the way to the end of the age. That means it must be within your lifetime... and maybe soon. The clouds are gathering and look more ominous every day. Like watching a storm coming across the ocean, you can see the clouds move closer; you can hear thunder and see the lightning. You feel the wind picking up and see the waves getting higher. If the storm represents God's judgment, then as soon as the storm is directly overhead, the Bride of Christ will be on her way to meet the Groom.

I hope this explanation is helpful to you. I will pray for you as you fulfill the destiny to which God has called you. I will leave you with the words God spoke to Joshua:

Be strong and courageous. Do not be terrified; do not be discouraged, for the LORD your God will be with you wherever you go (Joshua 1:9).

Write to me anytime. I am delighted to be a part of what God will be doing through you!

Yours in Christ, Sarah Foxworth

Chapter 24:

Lessons From the Tea Shop

It was 6:00 AM. Brian got up from the computer and couldn't wait to hear what Sarah would say about his dream. He decided to go back to bed. A long day was ahead, and more sleep was needed. Brian crept back into the room and slipped under the covers while trying not to wake up Maryanne, but she woke up anyway.

"Why are you up?" she asked.

"I had a dream… but now I need more sleep. Good night, Gorgeous."

She sighed and went back to sleep. She would need to get up in thirty minutes to help Hyler get ready for school. Brian would sleep until about 9:00.

He came down for breakfast. Maryanne was reading the latest news on her iPad. "Good morning, Mr. Michaels. Did you get enough sleep?"

"I hope so. Barcelona is a nine-hour flight."

"What is this dream you had?"

Brian decided not to go into a description of his dream yet. He would wait until Sarah could give him more perspective.

"I don't know. It was just very weird. It woke me up and I couldn't get back to sleep. I need to leave for the airport at around 4:00 this afternoon. Did you want to do something today before I go?"

"No, I have to work at the school again this afternoon. By the way, Hyler was very excited this morning about what happened last night. I think she put a note in your flight case. Can I read it with you?"

Brian went into the den, opened the case and found her note right on top. It was folded four times and had a big red heart on the outside with a cross in the middle. He brought it into the kitchen. Brian and Maryanne stood next to each other as he opened the note.

"Dad, I love you sooooooo much. I am sooooooo happy that we all believe in Jesus now. I really like it when you read me Bible stories. I hope you never stop. I will ask Mommy to read when you are gone. Have a safe trip!"

Mom and Dad both wiped away tears.

Maryanne raised her right hand and said, "Brian, I promise to read her Bible stories when you are gone. I know it's important... I also want to call the church and see what kind of Bible study I can join with other women. I need to figure out what this Christian life is all about."

"That means a lot to me, Honey. I love you sooooooo much too!"

Maryanne laughed.

Brian walked back into the den and checked his email; nothing from Sarah yet. Wives always like to see their husbands doing constructive things around the house so he decided to tackle the garage. It was going to be another nice day–good for cleaning and organizing.

Caught up in the activity, he didn't realize how fast the time had passed. "Are you ready for lunch?" Maryanne called out. A ham and cheese sandwich, a few chips, and a Diet Coke were waiting for him on the table. "Thanks dear," he said holding her around the waist and putting a gentle peck on her cheek. They sat together at the table while Maryanne scrolled on her iPhone and read to him the more insane headlines of the day. Brian blurted, half joking and half serious, "What is wrong with this world!" Then, putting on his best theatrical voice, "Its gone mad I tell you, mad!" Maryanne was laughing at him. A playful joy had filled their hearts. They were both tuned to the same frequency, not of the world, but of the kingdom.

After lunch, Maryanne left to volunteer at the school. Brian was again alone in the house but still had a few hours to kill.

Remembering a little teashop from the other night on their ice cream outing, he was reminded of all the quaint outdoor cafes in Italy. It was time to check it out. Taking the car this time, and packing the laptop, he headed back to the Avenue.

Walking in the door of Tea Fusions, he immediately sensed the sweet presence of the Spirit. Christian music played softly in the background. One wall was decorated with individual word signs representing the fruits of the spirit: *love, joy, peace, patience, kindness, goodness, faith, gentleness, and self-control.* Brian looked at the signs for a minute and realized that so many of those "fruits" had become alive in him only since Orvieto! He didn't just decide to be a better person, it was emanating from the core of his being where the Spirit of God now dwelled. It was a profound moment of understanding.

As he approached the front counter, a tall man with olive toned skin greeted him. "What can I do for you today?" he asked with a slight accent. "By the way, my name is Mo."

"I love your shop. It's very inviting. Your signs really moved me." Brian said as he pointed to the wall.

247

"Yes, in addition to wonderful teas we offer even better fruit." he said jokingly. "Of course, you know those are the fruits of the Spirit as mentioned in Galatians 5:22."

"Well, I wasn't sure exactly until just now. Thank you for being open with your witness!"

"When you are a direct descendant of the Prophet Mohammed and suddenly Jesus gets a hold of your life, it's hard not to be a witness. I was in darkness for a long time; being in the light is a lot better! I just try to keep the light shining in this humble teahouse. Have you had one of our teas before?"

"No, this is my first time here, what would you suggest?"

"We have a couple dozen teas all specially formulated. Divine Temple is very popular. It's a blend of six different green teas mixed with pineapple, mango, and orange peels. It will kick start your day!" Mo brought out a large canister, opened the lid and allowed Brian to smell the aroma.

"That smells wonderful!"

Mo was a master with tea and knew all the nuances of each blend. He was an expert with people too and Brian could tell he had a heart of gold. "This one is called Rose of the Orient and contains mango and rose petals."

"This one smells great too, my wife would love it. The only tea I've ever had before was from a tea bag. To smell and see all the ingredients is amazing" *This tea really is like smelling the roses.* Brian chuckled at the thought—it was an inside joke.

Mo loved educating his customers about all the blends. "This one is called To Life and is made with white tea, jasmine pearls, and rooibos from Cape Town, South Africa."

In our culture of fast or processed foods, it is a rare thing to see, smell and touch something so natural and earthy. It's like we live in a cocoon of artificiality. Mo was the master of teas, but God is the master of creation. It was more than the delightful scent of the different teas, but actually seeing the various herbs, berries, leaves and flowers comprising each distinctive blend was an immersion in color and texture. The vast variety revealed richness of God himself. All of creation emanated from the mind of the Creator. Seeing and smelling the teas stirred the same admiration he experienced in the nature preserve.

"There is one more I want you to see. It is called Sikkim, which means House of Snow. It is a rare black tea that grows at six thousand feet in the Himalayas." The aroma was deep and rich. "Which one would you like?"

"I'll try 'To Life'!" That one said it all.

249

Mo the tea master went to work. There were only a few other people in the restaurant. One looked like a college girl and was reading a Bible! You don't see that every day. There was freedom in this place. Bring a Bible out anywhere else and you would feel the eyes of everyone around. Here there was liberty. It stemmed from the ownership. Mo and his business partner Susan set the tone. They were determined to make sure Christ and those who follow him were welcome. Brian sat down to wait as the tea steeped for the required three minutes.

"Here you go sir, hope you enjoy your first cup of real tea."

A tall ceramic mug sat steaming in front of him. Its distinctive scent wafted up and across his face. Brian knew there was a message in all this. What new metaphor was God revealing? It wasn't the cup that captivated him; it was the aroma. Each tea formulation had its own distinctive blend of ingredients, creating a unique identity.

He thought of Sikkim and how it grew only in the mountains of India. The hardship of growing in rock and snow made it strong. If the cup represents our life, then the aroma must correspond to our personalities. As human beings, we are the unique sum of all our life experiences, from ethnic and racial background to birth order, economics, education, family, and so much more, some of it good and some of it bad.

Imagine the variables! God is not into bland. He loves variety, just look at all he has made!

The blend of our cultural and life experiences determines our unique flavor and aroma. Even our pain and suffering, like the Sikkim tea, makes us stronger… if we don't lose hope. Christ removes the impurities from our life, but it is our own commitment that determines whether we are hot, lukewarm, or cold. God wants to sample our cup and be pleased with its essence.

Brian sipped his tea. It was hot and wonderful. He whispered a prayer. "Lord let me always be like this cup of tea, hot for your Word and full of your Spirit. May I always offer an aroma pleasing to you and those around me, Amen."

Brian noticed the "Free Wi-Fi" sign in the window and jaunted out to the car to grab the laptop. Sitting back down with his tea, he checked his email. There it was! The message had come in only about five minutes earlier. The subject read, "About your dream."

Brian couldn't remember when he was in more anticipation about anything. The message itself was short. Brian was disappointed until he saw that there was a Word attachment.

Sarah's message read:

Brian,

I did this as quickly as I could and spent the whole afternoon working on it. God has given you a special mission to accomplish and a unique tool to do it with; The Chalice of Truth. A prosecutor will often talk of a criminal having the motive, means and opportunity to commit a crime. The same thing happens when we choose to do something for good instead of evil. Your motive is to reach those who are lost without faith, your means is the Chalice of Truth, and your opportunity is the freedom and flexibility you have as a pilot. May you exploit all three to accomplish great things for the kingdom. I hope the attached interpretation of your dream spurs you on. It is an amazing vision, and millions need to hear it. God will guide you. Stay in touch. Blessings to you and your family.

Yours in Christ, Sarah Foxworth

Brian opened the attachment and began to read. The purpose of his life came into focus.

Final Thought

Some people compare the Chalice of Truth to the Holy Grail. Perhaps there are similarities, it is not known if the original Communion cup used by Jesus still exists. In the end, it is not about finding an ancient artifact. Rather, it's about finding truth and sharing it with others while there is still time.

Maranatha!

Addendum

Use of "Oracle" in Scripture

The word "oracle" is used forty-four times in the Old Testament (NIV).

First use of the word "oracle" is with the prophet Balaam as recorded in Numbers 24:15

"*The oracle of Balaam son of Beor, the oracle of one whose eye sees clearly, the oracle of one who hears the words of God, who has knowledge from the Most High, who sees a vision from the Almighty, who falls prostrate, and whose eyes are opened.*"

From the prophet Samuel regarding King David:

These are the last words of David: "The oracle of David son of Jesse, the oracle of the man exalted by the Most High" (2 Sam 23:1).

From Isaiah:

An oracle concerning Damascus: "See, Damascus will no longer be a city but will become a heap of ruins" (Isa 17:1).

From Zechariah regarding Israel in the last days:

*An **Oracle**: This is the word of the LORD concerning Israel. The LORD, who stretches out the heavens, who lays the foundation of the earth, and who forms the spirit of man within him, declares: "I am going to make Jerusalem a cup that sends all the surrounding peoples reeling. Judah will be besieged as well as Jerusalem. On that day, when all the nations of the earth are gathered against her, I will make Jerusalem an immovable rock for all the nations. All who try to move it will injure themselves* (Zech 12:1-3).

Use of Creeds

The Apostle's Creed was probably first written down by the Apostles after Pentecost and before they set out on their missionary journeys, but it was adopted as a formal creed in the early fourth century. Creeds were used to combat heresy as doctrines of the trinity, the incarnation, the virgin birth, the resurrection, and the divinity of Christ were all under constant attack. The creed served as a plumb line for the faith. Despite what the DaVinci Code would have you believe, the divinity of Christ was a well-established doctrine by the end of the First Century. Paul incorporates part of an early creed in 1 Corinthians 15:3-7 written within thirty years of the events surrounding Christ.

Russ Breault

The Apostle's Creed

I believe in God,
the Father almighty,
Creator of heaven and earth,
and in Jesus Christ, his only Son, our Lord,
who was conceived by the Holy Spirit,
born of the Virgin Mary,
suffered under Pontius Pilate,
was crucified, died and was buried;
he descended into hell;
on the third day he rose again from the dead;
he ascended into heaven,
and is seated at the right hand of God the Father almighty;
from there he will come to judge the living and the dead.
I believe in the Holy Spirit,
the holy catholic (universal) Church,
the communion of saints,
the forgiveness of sins,
the resurrection of the body,
and life everlasting.
Amen.

A Prayer to Receive Christ

Dear Heavenly Father, I come to you admitting that I am a sinner. I ask for your forgiveness and with your help, I repent and turn away from sin and ask you to cleanse me from all unrighteousness. I believe that Your Son, Jesus, willingly died on the cross and shed His blood to take away my sins. I also believe that He rose again from the dead making a way for me to inherit the promise of eternal life. I call upon the name of Jesus Christ to be the Savior and Lord of my life. Jesus, I choose to follow you, and I ask that you fill me with the power of the Holy Spirit to guide and direct me the rest of my life. I declare right now that I am a born-again child of God, my sins are forgiven, and I am saved in Jesus' name. Thank you for coming into my life! Amen.

Author's Note

The Oracle of Orvieto is a work of fiction. It is, however, historically accurate as it relates to places, events, and famous figures. All the modern-day characters are fictional with perhaps some autobiographical elements included as it relates to the conversion experience. Saint Thomas Aquinas did live and teach in Orvieto; however, the author is not aware of him crafting a special chalice. It is a literary device for the purposes of the story. Saint Patrick's Well does exist as described and is considered an architectural wonder with its double helix stairway. However, the author is not aware of any spiritual encounters occurring there... but who knows? It also was used as a literary device. Three Fountains Abbey in Rome is a Trappist monastery as described. However, Father Vittorio Gabelli is a fictional character, though I would love to meet him! Peachtree City is a real community as described about 30 minutes South of the Atlanta airport. Tea Fusions was a lovely tea shop as described but it is no longer in business. However, it will always be in our hearts as a place of Christian connection run by Mo the tea master, a direct descendant of the Prophet Mohammed and Susan his business partner. Together they would open their establishment on Sunday nights for a Bible study. It was at one of these meetings when I led a study on the many ways the word "cup" is used in the Bible. A woman attended that night who had never been there before. Afterwards, she came up to me and said, "You should write a book about that." She never came back, and I never saw her again. I was quite taken by her statement and was surprised that she would suggest an entire book could be written about a cup. This occurred around the same time that a Christian book based on a fictional story became a nationwide bestseller. That is how and when The Oracle of Orvieto began to take shape, as a fictional story to reveal the deep truths of Scripture, and especially the cup as a unique metaphor for how the Trinity works in our lives; God makes the cup, Jesus cleans the cup, and the Holy Spirit fills the cup… hopefully to overflowing. Many thanks are offered to many people who helped make this book a reality, but it all started with a humble tea shop and the proprietors who created such a faith-filled environment.

About the Author

Russ Breault is an international expert on the Shroud of Turin, Christianity's most analyzed artifact, believed by millions to be the burial cloth that wrapped Jesus in the tomb. He is the founder of the Shroud of Turin Education Project, Inc. and travels worldwide bringing his highly acclaimed big screen presentation known as "Shroud Encounter" to college, university and church audiences. He has appeared in numerous documentaries along with national interview shows and is the author of *Shroud Encounter: Explore the World's Greatest Unsolved Mystery*. He can be contacted through his website, www.ShroudEncounter.com.

The Oracle of Orvieto is his first published work of fiction.

Made in the USA
Monee, IL
22 July 2025